Marion Lennox has written over one hundred romance novels, and is published in over one hundred countries and thirty languages. Her international awards include the prestigious RITA® award (twice!) and the *RT Book Reviews* Career Achievement Award for 'a body of work which makes us laugh and teaches us about love'. Marion adores her family, her kayak, her dog, and lying on the beach with a book someone else has written. Heaven!

Also by Marion Lennox

Meant-To-Be Family
From Christmas to Forever?
Saving Maddie's Baby
A Child to Open Their Hearts
Falling for Her Wounded Hero
Stranded with the Secret Billionaire
Reunited with Her Surgeon Prince
The Billionaire's Christmas Baby
Finding His Wife, Finding a Son
English Lord on Her Doorstep

Discover more at millsandboon.co.uk.

THE BABY THEY LONGED FOR

MARION LENNOX

MILLS & BOON

First published in Great Britain 2019
by Mills & Boon, an imprint of HarperCollins*Publishers*
1 London Bridge Street, London, SE1 9GF

Large Print edition 2019

© 2019 Marion Lennox

ISBN: 978-0-263-07837-4

FLINTSHIRE SIR Y FFLINT		
C29 0000 1197 164		ntly certified nanagement. For 1s.co.uk/green.
		itain
MAGNA	£16.99	CR0 4YY

CHAPTER ONE

HAPPY IS THE bride the sun shines on.

Happier still was the bride's mother.

Addie's mum had been beaming ever since she'd read the weather forecast. Actually, she'd been beaming from the moment Addie and Gavin had announced their engagement.

Dr Adeline Blair should be beaming, too, but right now she was struggling. In truth, Addie seemed so far away from her normal, workaday self it was like she'd moved into another body.

She didn't belong…here?

Why? Surely everything was perfect. She was about to marry her childhood sweetheart. She was making her mother gloriously happy. With luck, she and Gavin might even have a baby before…

Don't go there. Not today.

She glanced sideways at her mum, sitting beside her in the bridal limousine. Cancer.

Metastases. Maeve seemed well today, but tomorrow…

No.

'This is the happiest day of my life,' Maeve breathed, and Addie hugged her—which, considering the amount of tulle she was wearing, plus the weight of her over-the-top veil, took some doing.

The car pulled to a stop. The church looked picture-postcard perfect. An arch of roses framed the entrance. Guests were presumably tucked up inside, waiting for the arrival of the bride. A photographer stood ready.

Addie had no extra attendants, no bridesmaids. Her mother was being bridal attendant as well as giving her away, an all-in-one package.

In some ways, it was almost her mother's wedding.

'Oh, Addie.' As the chauffeur opened the car doors, her mother's eyes were like stars. 'I can't believe this is happening.'

And Addie finally relaxed. Her mother was happy. Gavin was waiting. She knew she loved him—she always had. The reservations that had prevented this happening years ago were surely dumb.

This was as good as she could make it.

But then…

She lifted the load of tulle from around her ankles, swung herself out of the car—and straight into Noah McPherson.

Noah. Surgical consultant at Sydney Central. Gavin's immediate boss.

Gav's best man.

Noah was tall, dark and imposing in his beautifully cut dinner suit. He was in his early thirties but his skill and gravitas made him seem older. Addie saw lots of gravitas now.

Why wasn't he with Gav?

'What's…what's wrong?' she managed, but she knew almost before she spoke.

'Gav can't do it.'

'Can't do…what?'

She couldn't believe this. She was standing in brilliant sunshine, in her fairy-floss dress, and she was asking a question she already knew the answer to. She'd known the answer since she'd seen Noah.

'Gav says he can't marry you,' Noah said, quite gently. 'I'm so sorry.'

Silence.

There should be bells, Addie thought, almost hysterically. Her mother and Gav's mother had organised bell-ringers. Addie had paid for them.

Maybe the bells had moved to her head. She felt like it was about to explode.

Gavin was…*jilting her*? This wasn't real. It didn't happen.

It couldn't happen.

'I… Did he give you any explanation?' She was weirdly proud that she'd got the question out without gibbering.

'He did. But you don't want to hear it now.'

'Tell me,' she commanded.

Whoa…

Once upon a time Adeline Blair had had a temper, but not now. She'd had years of living in a house where every outburst would be greeted with, 'Oh, Addie, what would your father say? You'll break my heart even more.' Her mother's tears had pretty much shoved Addie's temper into a dark cellar, tethered it with chains and left it to its own devices.

But right now she could feel the chains snapping. 'Tell me,' she hissed again, and Noah flinched.

'Addie, we can do this later. We can find somewhere private—'

'I need to know now. Tell me why.'

He took a deep breath and visibly braced. 'Gav said…all his life he's been ruled by women. Their grief and their need. And now your mum's ill… He couldn't tell you. He didn't wish you—or your mother or his—any more unhappiness, but he's decided that he can't keep on being needed. He wants his own life.'

'His own life.'

'That's what he said.'

'So he's decided…' Temper or not, she was struggling to find her voice. She had to try a couple of times before she succeeded. 'He decided to wait to tell me until five minutes before he was due to marry me? And then he didn't even tell me himself?' She was fighting rising hysteria. Stay calm, she told herself, but herself refused to listen.

'I guess… Look, would you like me to drive you anywhere?'

'Go jump,' she hissed. 'He didn't even have the courage to phone?'

'He thought you'd talk him out of it.' He considered his words. 'Or into it. Whatever.'

'He sees me as what...the enemy?'

'Maybe you need to see it from his point of view.' It seemed like Noah was trying to make this whole scenario logical. 'He says you depend on him. He doesn't want to hurt you, but he feels like he's been blackmailed by your mother's illness. By your need.'

What the... 'He w-wants to m-marry me,' she stammered. 'He's been asking me almost once a week since I was seven.'

'Maybe he thought you'd never say yes. I don't know. All I know is that he's finally realised that he can't go through with it. He says he can't be controlled any more by what he calls...'

'What he calls what?' She didn't recognise herself. She didn't recognise the anger.

'Addie...'

'What d-did he call me?' Addie stammered.

'Not only you. I think it's you, your mum, his mum.'

'So what did he call...*us*?'

'This isn't helpful.'

'Say it.'

He sighed—and then he said it. 'He called you...a monstrous regiment of women.'

Silence.

People were starting to make their way out of the church, wondering what was happening. Rebecca was way out front. Rebecca was Noah's wife, wheelchair bound and beautiful beyond belief. She was also the source of any vitriolic hospital gossip she could find. Right now her face was alive with speculation. Pleasure?

All their hospital friends were behind her.

Gavin's mum was with them. Lorna looked appalled.

Her mum was beside her, looking ashen.

'You've been with Gav for the entire morning, listening to this drivel,' Addie managed at last, struggling to keep her voice from being heard by anyone else. 'He doesn't want to be needed? I've cared for his mum as well as mine, for as long as I can remember. And now... You

work with me and you didn't even have the de-
cency to warn me...'

The chains were definitely snapped now, and
her package of temper, bundled up and controlled for all these years, was suddenly running amuck. All she could see was crimson.

'Addie, I'm sorry.'

'Of course you're sorry,' she said, distantly
now. 'That's why everyone's heading this way.
Everyone's sorry. Oh, and here's Rebecca, ready
to soak up every detail. Explain it to your wife,
will you. And everyone else. A monstrous regiment of women? His mum? My mum? Me?'

'Addie...' He put a hand on her shoulder.

And then Adeline Blair did what she'd never
done in her life and would never do again.

She struck his hand, and, as he didn't release
her, she shoved away. And as he instinctively
held on—to comfort, maybe, who knew?—she
reached out and slapped his smug, sorry face, a
slap so hard the sound rang out over the church-
yard to the town beyond.

And Dr Adeline Blair, dutiful daughter, dot-
ing fiancée, or ex-fiancée, jilted bride—oh,
and obstetrician as well—hitched up her bridal

gown, tugged off her veil and kicked off her stupid satin shoes.

'Look after Mum,' she called over her shoulder to Gavin's mother, because even then she was a dutiful daughter.

And then she ran.

CHAPTER TWO

Three years later

'WE'RE VERY GLAD to welcome you to the staff. Six months is great. Have you seen enough of the hospital? Terrific set-up, isn't it? Let's show you to the doctors' residence and get you settled.'

Noah had looked at this place on the internet and liked what he'd seen. Now, in reality, the hospital met his expectations and more. It was small but it seemed excellent.

Currawong Bay was two hours' drive from Sydney, tucked between mountains and sea on New South Wales' south coast. It was a hazardous drive to the next major medical centre, or a fast helicopter flight if weather conditions permitted, so the hospital was geared to independence. For the last few weeks that independence had been compromised. They'd been lacking a surgeon.

Luckily the role of temporary surgeon was a job Noah needed. It was six months before his court case could be heard. Until then he had no access to his daughter.

No. Seven-year-old Sophie was not his daughter, he told himself, for what must surely be the thousandth time. She was the daughter of his ex-wife and he had no legal claim.

But how could he stop caring for a child he'd loved since she was a toddler? He couldn't, which was why he'd needed to leave Sydney. He needed a busy, hands-on workload to keep him sane.

'There's only one other occupant in our doctors' house.' Henry, the hospital's middle-aged administrator, was bluff and genial. 'But the house is good. Because of our isolation we're often dependent on locums, and this helps attract them. The place is set up to give privacy. It's right on site. You can share the living rooms, or stick to your own rooms if you wish to be by yourself.'

'Who's living there now?' He hadn't planned on sharing at all. The advertisement had said self-contained quarters. How did that fit?

'Our obstetrician.' Henry seemed oblivious to his qualms. 'She's been here for almost three years now and because of the nature of her work the doctors' house is a good fit. Hopefully she'll be home now. Come through and I'll introduce you.'

But then Henry's phone rang. He took the call, glancing out at the gorgeous day outside. When the call ended he sighed but the sigh didn't sound too unhappy. 'Sorry, Noah, but there's been a hitch. One of my golfing mates forgot his anniversary tonight, so tee off has been brought forward.'

It was Saturday afternoon. The bay was a glistening sheet of sapphire, the golf course lying enticingly in the distance. This had to be one of the most beautiful places for a hospital in the world. Henry's choice was obvious.

'If you head down the veranda and across the walkway, third door on your left, you'll find everything you need,' he said hurriedly. 'You're expected. Introduce yourself and make yourself at home. Settle in, explore the bay, do what you want until we start throwing work at you on Monday. By the way, do you play golf? No? Shame. Gotta go, though. Welcome to Currawong.'

He was gone and Noah was left to his own devices.

Which suited him fine.

He walked out to the veranda and took a few moments to soak in the view. This was a good decision, he thought. A busy country hospital in a beautiful place. All types of surgery. A great place to live until the courts came down on his side.

Please…

Meanwhile he had a housemate.

That wasn't great. He'd prefer to be by himself. He needed to get his head sorted.

To prepare himself for losing Sophie?

He walked slowly along the veranda, taking time to appreciate the wicker armchairs set out for recuperating patients to sit in the sun and admire the view to the beach beyond. The doctors' accommodation was linked to the hospital by a breezeway, a separate house, simple, wooden, with wide French windows opening to the sea.

A window at the far end was open, the curtains wafting out in the breeze.

He reached the door, raised his hand to knock and then paused.

A moan… Stifled. Coming from the window at the end.

Was his housemate ill?

Knocking and demanding entrance if she was vomiting didn't seem such a great idea.

The glass doors led to what looked like a living room. No one was inside. He tried the door and found it unlocked.

The house was old-fashioned, furnished for comfort rather than style, with high ceilings, worn wooden floors and faded rugs. The living room was full of overstuffed furniture, big, comfortable, homey.

A vase of crimson poppies sat on the sideboard. They still had a band around their stems, looking like whoever had put them in the vase hadn't had the energy to let them free. He looked around, liking what he saw—and then there was another groan.

Uh-oh. This wasn't a gastro-type groan. He'd been a doctor long enough to differentiate.

This was pain. Sharp pain.

And even as he thought it, the door opened. A woman stood framed in the doorway, slight, mousy-brown hair, heavy glasses, wearing a faded nightgown.

Clutching her stomach.

'Who—?' She stopped at what was obviously her bedroom door and seemed to gather strength. 'Who...?'

'I'm Noah McPherson.' He frowned with concern. She was bending with pain, and while he watched, one hand went from her stomach to her shoulder. 'Surgeon.'

'Surgeon,' she gasped. And then she paused and tried to focus. 'Oh, hell... Noah?'

And he got it. He'd worked with her. He'd watched her as a jilted bride. She'd slapped him, hard.

'Addie,' he said blankly.

But she was no longer listening. She was clutching her side, focussing inward. 'Noah...' She struggled to find words. 'Oh, help. Noah, I don't want... Of all the people... But I think

I need...' Her knees seemed to buckle and she dropped to a crouch.

And any confusion he was feeling faded in the face of medical need. He stooped before her, pushing the tangle of curls back from her eyes. 'What's happening? Addie, tell me.'

'I think... No, I know that I'm pregnant,' she gasped, struggling to breathe. 'Test...positive. Ten weeks. I haven't had an ultrasound yet but now...pain like you wouldn't believe. My shoulder hurts. And... I've started... I've started to bleed. I've had...endometriosis. It's a risk and these are classic symptoms. I think my pregnancy's ectopic. I want her so much. Oh, Noah, I'm losing my baby.'

His brief tour of the hospital with Henry had been enough for him to find the right people, fast, and without exception Currawong Bay's nursing staff were appalled.

No one seemed to have guessed Addie was pregnant. From the orderly who came running to help him get her across to the hospital, to the nurses, even to the hospital cook who appeared from the kitchen because she couldn't believe what she'd just heard, they were horrified.

Noah was horrified himself, but he had to put his dismay on the backburner. The hospital used the town's family doctors as backup. They could care for their own patients when they were in hospital, but it seemed none had specific surgical training.

If this was indeed an ectopic pregnancy, then this was his call.

'I need…a scan,' Addie breathed as they wheeled her along the veranda.

'I'm onto it,' he told her. He touched her face, lightly, in an attempt at reassurance. 'Addie, let me do the worrying. You know I'm a surgeon. I might not know as much as you do about pregnancy complications but I know enough to cope with this. Trust me?'

'I… Yes.' And she caught his hand. For a moment he thought it was to push it away but instead it turned into a death grip as more pain hit. 'I don't…have a choice.'

She didn't. It was, indeed, an ectopic pregnancy.

A scan showed an embryo growing in the

right fallopian tube rather than the womb. Such pregnancies were doomed from the start, and internal bleeding was now threatening her life.

He didn't have to explain it to Addie. She watched the screen with him, her face racked with distress. Pain relief was kicking in. The nurses were prepped, the theatre was ready but they were waiting for the anaesthetist. Apparently he was on his way, pulled from his son's football game.

'I wanted this baby so much,' she breathed. 'Oh, Noah... I have endometriosis. Scarring. If the other tube's damaged...'

She'd know the odds. Rupture meant an increased risk of future infertility, and if she already suffered from endometriosis the odds were even worse. It was a hard call, treating a doctor, Noah thought. It was impossible to reassure her when she knew the facts.

She'd also know that he was a second-best doctor right now. What she needed was a specialist obstetrician, and the hospital had only one. Addie.

But if Noah hadn't decided to come a couple of days early there wouldn't be any surgeon within an hour's reach. For the first time Noah was hit with the drama of country medical practice. Him or no one.

'Please...' Addie was weeping in her distress. Once more her hand caught his. 'I know I've lost my baby but I can't...please, I can't be infertile.'

'I'll do what I can,' he said gently. 'Addie, you know I can make no promises.' He was administering pre-meds, willing the unknown anaesthetist to hurry.

'You can repair the tube.' Her voice was blurred from the drugs and pain and shock. 'You must. Please.'

He knew he couldn't. So must she if she was thinking straight. If they'd caught things before the rupture then maybe but now...

'Addie, you know...'

'I do,' she whispered. 'But please... I'm sorry I slapped you.'

And that made him smile. Of all things to be thinking... 'If I'd been you that day, I might have slapped me, too.'

'It should have been Gav.' She took a deep breath, fighting for strength, but there was still spirit. 'To let me get to the church… Toe rags, both of you.'

'We were indeed toe rags,' he said gravely. 'Addie, is there anyone we should be contacting? You need some support. Your mum?' He hesitated. 'The baby's father?'

'No.' It was a harsh snap.

He wanted to stop but he had to know. Addie was suffering internal bleeding. Where the hell was the anaesthetist? If they didn't get in soon… 'Addie, we need next of kin at least.'

'Next of kin's this baby.'

'Addie…'

'There's no one,' she snapped. 'Mum died three years ago. Gav's mother doesn't speak to me, and Gav's long gone. And this baby's father is a number from a sperm bank. So if I die on the operating table feel free to donate everything to the local cats' home. But, oh, Noah…' Her voice shattered on a sob and her grip on his hand tightened. He was no friend but he knew her from the past and it seemed that right now he was all she had.

'You will… The tubes… You will try.'

'I will.'

'Despite the slap.'

'Maybe even a little because of the slap,' he said ruefully. 'You were treated appallingly that day.'

And then he looked up as a redheaded beanpole burst through the door.

'Hey,' the beanpole said, heading for Noah and holding out his hand in greeting. 'You'll be our new surgeon. Noah? I'm Cliff Brooks, anaesthetist.' He grasped Noah's hand and then turned his attention to the patient. And stilled in shock. 'What the...? Addie!'

'It's ectopic,' Addie said weakly. 'I'm... I was... Oh, Cliff, it's ectopic.'

'Bugger,' Cliff said, and then added a couple more expletives for good measure. 'We didn't even know... I'm so sorry, love.' He then proceeded to be entirely unprofessional by stooping and giving Addie a hug.

'Hell, Ad, this is the pits but don't worry. I'll be watching our new surgeon every step of the way. Let's get you into Theatre and get things cleared. And if you want to be pregnant... This'll just be a blip. Maryanne had two miscarriages before she had Michael, and now we have four boys. Hiccups are what happens when you start a family. Don't cry, love, don't cry.'

So he hugged and Noah turned away and headed for the sinks. He felt like he'd felt on Addie's wedding day. Helpless. And…he had no right to comfort her, so why did it seem so wrong that it wasn't him who did the hugging?

An ectopic pregnancy was always a grief. Growing in the fallopian tubes instead of in the womb, there was no chance a baby could survive. Someday someone might figure a way such a pregnancy could be transplanted to the womb, Noah thought, but that day was a long way off.

By the time of the rupture, the embryo was lifeless. The pressure was on to save the mother. Preserving fertility had to come second. When a woman had a complete family and there was no need to try and make future pregnancies viable, the surgery was much simpler but now… Noah was calling on skills he barely had.

Cliff was good. Noah had checked out the credentials of his anaesthetist before taking on the job, but he'd never worked with him. The fact that he was personally involved could have been a worry, but from the moment he'd released Addie from the hug Cliff had turned pure professional.

'You focus on your end. Leave everything else to me,' Cliff growled, and at least Noah could stop thinking about blood pressure, about the logistics of keeping a haemorrhaging patient alive, and focus purely on the technical.

Except he couldn't quite, because this was Addie.

Separation of personal to professional…how hard was that? He'd glanced at Cliff as Addie had slipped under, and he'd seen grimness in the man's expression. He wasn't the only one caught in personal distress for the woman they were operating on.

But why did he feel like this?

In truth he'd only had a working relationship, with Gavin as well as Addie. He'd been Gavin's boss but he'd been surprised to be asked to be best man. Gavin had obviously kept his life compartmentalised. Work, home and stuff-that-no-one-was-to-know-about. Until after the wedding fiasco when the hospital grapevine had practically exploded.

Addie had kept to herself, too, but where Gavin's lesser-known compartment had turned out to be spectacular, Addie's seemed anything but. The grapevine said that she worked and she looked after her mother. At the hospital she and Noah had occasionally operated or consulted together, but he'd thought her quiet, almost mousy. Technically skilled. Conscientious. Nothing special.

He'd operated on colleagues before, men and women he'd known far better than this. So now…why was it so hard to block out the thought of Addie's distress, the sight of her face, bleached by fear and shock?

He had to block it out. Her life depended on it.

The first part of the surgery was straightforward. An incision, finding the source of the bleeding, removing the unviable pregnancy. There was inflammation around it, and bleeding from the rupture.

'Possible to do a salpingotomy?' Cliff queried as Noah cleared and tried to see what he was left with.

Salpingotomy was the removal of the damaged embryo and then microscopic repair and preservation of the fallopian tube. He looked at the damage under his hands and shook his head. Such microscopic surgery took real obstetric skill, skills he wasn't sure he possessed. There wasn't time to transfer her to Sydney for a specialist obstetric surgeon to take over, but even if there had been...

'Not possible,' he growled. 'There's too much damage to preserve it.' It had to be a salpingectomy, the complete removal of the tube. 'Future fertility rates aren't so different,' he muttered, talking to himself rather than to Cliff.

Cliff gave him a searching look and then nodded and went back to his monitors.

There was the sound of a sob from somewhere behind him—from one of the nurses.

So Addie was loved? She'd been working in this hospital for three years. A small hospital where people had come to know her.

He worked on, but as he did he was increasingly aware of the tension around him.

'We didn't even know she was pregnant,' the theatre nurse, Heidi, a woman in her fifties, muttered as he completed the removal of the damaged tube. 'There's never been a hint of a guy. She's been going back and forth to Sydney but only ever overnight. She never takes holidays. We thought…' She swallowed, biting back what she thought. 'The other tube?'

'Looks good,' he muttered, and felt a ripple of relief through the theatre.

'It's still awful.' Heidi was still looking distressed. 'Chances of successful pregnancy after…'

'It's better than death,' Cliff said roughly. 'The chances aren't zero. Leave it, Heidi. We all need to be positive, for Addie's sake.'

Noah was closing, carefully ensuring everything that could be done was done. If he'd been able to preserve the tube Addie would be facing constant monitoring over the next few weeks, to ensure there was no further growth in the tube, but at least now it was straightforward.

She'd recover. She'd get on with life.

Just as she had after the wedding, he thought.

Just as she had after being humiliated to the socks, standing jilted at a church with everyone she loved around her.

Everyone she loved?

Who loved Addie?

It was none of his business, he told himself. Addie was now a recovering patient. His patient. He needed to invoke professional detachment.

Like that was going to happen.

Cliff was reversing the anaesthetic. Heidi was leaning over Addie, ready to reassure her the minute she came around. A couple of other nurses stood in the background, looking distressed and concerned.

These were her people now. They were…all she had?

Regardless, they were here for her. He, on the other hand, was part of a nightmare from a distant past, and now he'd be part of today's nightmare.

He stepped away from the table, feeling almost light-headed. There was nothing else he could do.

'I'll leave her to you,' he told the staff. 'I…

Look after her. Constant obs. Don't leave her for a moment. I'll check back in an hour or so but I'm on the end of the phone if I'm needed before then.'

'Yeah, you need to unpack and settle,' Cliff said, roughly though, and Noah knew how deeply all those around the table were affected. 'Thanks, mate. You don't know how grateful we are that you were here for us.'

Us?

He looked down again at Addie and thought, This is your family. The hospital staff.

It was all she had?

Why did that feel so bad?

'Do you have everything you need?' Heidi asked, and he pulled himself together.

'Yes. Thank you. I won't be far away. Keep continual obs on her until I say not.' He'd already said it but it seemed important to say it again. She couldn't be left alone.

'Of course we will,' Heidi told him, and turned back to Addie. Noah was free to go.

After cleaning up post-op, he walked out onto the veranda and then further, out to the cliffs overlooking the beach.

Addie had lost her baby.

A baby...

Sophie...

For a moment he felt so dizzy he thought he'd be ill.

How could he ever have thought he could get away from this grief through work? He should have taken a job as a street cleaner for six months. Anything.

To lose a child...

'Get a grip,' he told himself, fiercely, as if it was important to make himself hear. 'You can't stop being a doctor because you've lost...'

'I haven't lost. Not yet.'

It felt like he had. Where was Sophie now? If he didn't win...

'Move on,' he told himself harshly. 'One step in front of the other, for as long as it takes.'

The grief was with her almost before she woke, almost before she remembered why she was grieving. It washed across her like a great black wave, swallowing all.

'Hey.' Heidi was holding her hand. 'Hey, Addie. You're okay.'

'My baby… I've lost…'

'Oh, Addie, we're so sorry. Yes, you've lost the baby but our new surgeon was wonderful. He's so skilled. He thinks…we all think that things will be fine.'

Fine. She let the word roll around her head as reality seeped back.

Noah was here, and he thought things were fine.

She should have hit him harder.

He unpacked, headed back out to the veranda and thought about a walk, but first he needed to check on Addie again. She should be on the other side of the anaesthetic, and the reality of what had happened would be sinking in.

There'd been no call from the nurses so things must be okay physically. But not only had she lost her baby, she'd know the chances of future pregnancies were now reduced. Future pregnancies weren't impossible but it'd be a concern adding to the grief of her loss.

The nurses would look after her. They knew her and cared for her. As for him… He'd been there when she'd been jilted. He'd been there when she'd lost her baby. He was someone she could well never wish to see again, he conceded, but she might have questions. He owed it to her to answer them if she did.

To lose a child… If someone could answer *his* questions…

Don't go there, he told himself savagely. He needed to block it. This was all about Addie.

He headed back into the hospital and a young nurse turned from the phone at the front desk, greeting him with relief.

'Mr McPherson. We were hoping you might not have left the hospital. We have a ten-year-old coming in from down the coast. He fell trying to reach a bird's nest and his dad thinks he's broken his leg. He should be here in about twenty minutes. I know you're not supposed to start until Monday, but seeing you're here…'

So much for taking the weekend to get acclimatised, he thought ruefully. Work started now.

But…was work Addie?

Professionally only, he told himself.

He'd come to Currawong Bay to put a failed

marriage behind him and to cope with an interminable wait. And Addie? Had she come here for the same reason? If so, the last person she'd want to see would be him, but for now he was her doctor. She'd have to wear it. She'd had enough pain today to mean the little more his presence added shouldn't make too much difference.

Addie lay back on the pillows and stared at the ceiling and thought…blank.

Nothing, nothing and nothing.

She might have known it would never work. For the last few weeks she'd been gloriously, ridiculously happy. The first twinges of morning sickness had been met with joy. She was going to be part of a family.

Admittedly it'd be a very small family—one mother and one baby—but it would be a family nonetheless. Here, in this hospital, she had the support around her to make it happen. This was a lovely little community and they'd welcomed her with open arms. There was one grumpy nurse administrator but she'd even been able to manoeuvre that into a working relationship. In the three years she'd been here she'd helped deliver countless babies, she'd made good friends, and she knew she could count on the staff and the community to help her.

Except now she wouldn't need them. Her hands fell to her tummy, to the wad of dressing where a tiny bump had been before, and she felt her eyes fill with tears.

She wouldn't cry. She never cried, not when Gavin had jilted her, not when her mum had died, not ever.

Oh, but her baby...

'Can I come in?' It was a light tap and Noah McPherson was at the door.

Of all the people to see her cry... Noah. She swiped the tears from her face and fought for dignity. The surge of anger she'd felt as she'd emerged from the anaesthetic had faded. It wasn't his fault Gavin had jilted her. It wasn't his fault she'd lost her baby.

He was a doctor, nothing more.

A doctor she'd hit. On top of everything else she was now cringing with remembered humiliation.

'Of course,' she managed. The junior nurse who'd been sitting beside her looked a query at Noah and then slipped away, leaving her alone with a man...who'd saved her life?

A man she'd hit.

'They tell me...you did a good job,' she said, struggling to find words. 'The best you could.'

'Addie, I'm so sorry you've lost your baby.'

He didn't need to be sympathetic. She didn't want him to be sympathetic.

She wanted her mum. Anyone. No one.

Not Noah.

'It's okay.'

'I'm very sure it's not,' he said gently. 'I can't imagine how you're feeling. Can I sit down?'

'I... Of course.' What else was there to say?

He sat on the chair the nurse had just vacated. For a moment she thought he was intending to reach out and take her hand and she hauled it under the covers pre-emptively. She saw him wince.

'I need to talk to you as your doctor,' he told her. 'That's all. Can you stand it?'

'Of...of course I can.'

He nodded, gravely. 'There's not a lot of good news but there is some. Addie…your baby… You know it was tragic chance that she started developing in the fallopian tube.'

'She?' she whispered. *Her baby…*

'That's an assumption,' he said gravely. 'I thought you said her. Am I right?'

'I did…think of her as a girl,' she said grudgingly, and her hands felt the dressing again. 'I… I know it's dumb but I was already thinking… Rose for my grandmother? But that's crazy.'

'It's not crazy at all,' he said gently. 'Rose. That's who she was. She was real, a baby who sadly started growing where she had no chance of survival.'

She could hardly speak. *She. Her baby.* He'd even said her name, a name that she'd almost felt silly for dreaming of. And for some reason it helped. For the last few weeks, filled with wonder and anticipation, she'd been talking to the tiny bump she could scarcely feel. And, yes, she knew she was a girl. At some primeval level…

Or was that because she had so little knowledge of boys? Her family had always been women. Well, two women, herself and her mum.

So many emotions… She wasn't thinking straight. The anaesthetic was still making its effects felt. She lay back on the pillows and closed her eyes.

'Addie…'

'Mmm…' She wanted to be left alone, in her cocoon of grief. Life felt…barren. She wanted… She wanted…

'Addie, let's talk practicalities,' Noah said, strongly now, and regardless of what she wanted he reached out and took her hand. He held it strongly, a warm, firm hold, the reassurance of one human being touching another. She didn't want it but, oh…she needed it. She should pull away but she didn't. Practicalities? Something solid?

Something solid like Noah, she thought, and his hand…helped.

'We might be able to preserve your embryo for burial if that's what you wish,' Noah told her. 'It'll need to go to Pathology but after that… There might be something. If you wish.'

'I…' It was something. Something to hold to. The remnants of her dream? A place to mourn? 'I do wish.'

'Then I'll try to make it happen. No promises but I'll do my best. For now, though, Addie, can we talk through the results of the surgery? Or do you want to leave it until later?'

'Now.' It was scarcely a whisper. How hard was this?

'Then I need to tell you that I had to remove the entire tube,' he told her, in that gentle but professional voice that was somehow what she needed. 'It was ruptured, and even if I'd managed to suture it, chances are there'd be microscopic embryonic tissue I couldn't remove, tissue that might cause even more problems in the future. So that's grim news. But, Addie, I checked the other tube and it's perfect. Perfect, Addie.'

'It doesn't mean…' She stopped. Her words had been a whisper and they faded out, but he knew what she'd been about to say.

'It doesn't mean future pregnancies are assured,' he finished for her. 'We both know that.

But it does mean future pregnancies are possible. More than possible. You need to give yourself a couple of months to let your body heal, and let yourself heal, too, but then there's no reason why you shouldn't try again.'

He saw her face close in pain. This was one of the hardest conversations…talking about a future pregnancy when she'd barely started her grieving over this one. But this was his job, laying out the facts. The facts needed to be implanted, to be there when she needed them.

'You're an obstetrician,' he said gently. 'You know the odds better than I do, but for now you don't need to think of them. Put them away for later. For now, just focus on you, on what you need, and on your grief for your tiny daughter.'

'You sound like you think she was real?'

'Isn't she real, Addie? Your Rose?'

He watched her face. This was the hardest part, he thought.

He remembered past lectures, dry as dust, the technicalities of surgical removal of ectopic pregnancies. But he'd sat in the lectures and looked at the diagrams of the baby developing in the fallopian tubes and he'd thought…

it involved a death. A loss. A grief. No matter what happened to cause the end of a pregnancy, there must still be grief. He'd understood it then, he'd had it enforced later from harsh, brutal experience and now, watching Addie's face, he knew it even more strongly.

'She was…my daughter,' she whispered. 'For such a short time.'

'And she was loved,' he said gently. 'And she'll always be a part of you. But for now…' The look of strain on her face was almost unbearable. 'You need to sleep. Do what your body tells you, Addie. The nurse will be coming back. If you need anything more, I'm within calling distance.'

'I… I know,' she muttered. 'Oh, Noah… I slapped you.'

'You're welcome to slap me again if it helps,' he told her, and smiled. 'Anything you want, just not as long as it stops you sleeping.' And then he paused. Someone had knocked on the ward door. A head poked around, Henry, the hospital administrator, his face puckered in concern. Things must be pretty bad to haul him from his golf, Noah thought, but as he surged into the room he remembered the distress on the faces of the theatre staff and he knew that Addie was indeed loved.

It made him feel better—sort of—but it also made him feel…bleak.

Why? He wasn't sure. But Henry was stooping to give Addie a careful kiss and the feeling of bleakness intensified.

'I'll leave you to Henry,' he managed. 'No more than five minutes, though, Henry, and the nurse needs to return before you leave. Addie needs to sleep.'

'She needs to sleep for months,' Henry said roundly. 'We've been telling her and telling her. Long weekends, that's all she'll ever take. Cliff rang me and I was never more shocked. Yes, I know it's hard to get staff to cover but, Addie, you now have no choice. We're running you out of town. Dr McPherson's shown he's more than capable of dealing with obstetric drama and we'll put in a call for an emergency locum to cover for you. You're heading to Sydney or wherever you want, maybe the Gold Coast, maybe further north, the Great Barrier Reef, somewhere you can lie in the sun for a couple of months and let your body recover.'

'A couple of months!' Addie sounded horrified.

'Absolutely,' Henry told her. 'At a quick calculation, you're due for nine weeks' leave, plus sick leave. So we're not taking no for an answer. My family has an apartment overlooking the beach on the Gold Coast if you want, or you could choose an alternative. Just not here. Addie, you could almost learn to play golf in two months. There's a life skill. But rest is paramount. Isn't that right, Dr McPherson?'

'You do need to rest,' Noah concurred.

'There. It's all settled. No argument. The nurses are out there planning and Morvena's already contacting locums. For the next few weeks we don't need you.'

And then Heidi appeared in the doorway with meds and Henry turned to Heidi and started discussing the pros and cons of Gold Coast versus Great Barrier Reef and it was time for Noah to back away. From her...family?

'Two more minutes and then sleep,' he said

warningly, and got a nod of distracted agreement from Heidi and Henry.

Addie didn't need him any more. He was free
to go.

Free.

That was what he had to get used to.

CHAPTER THREE

Two months later

SHE SHOULD HAVE moved on. Maybe she should have started a new life altogether, but she'd already been there, done that, got the T-shirt.

A two-month break had changed a lot of things. But she knew she could move forward in Currawong.

During the whole time she'd been convalescing, the hospital staff, the Currawong mums she'd delivered, sometimes seemingly the whole community, had kept in touch as much as she wanted.

Currawong felt like home.

There was the hitch that Noah McPherson would still be living in the doctors' quarters. He'd been with her during two of the worst moments in her life. His presence made her feel... vulnerable.

She'd slapped him when he'd been nothing but a messenger for Gavin's cowardly retreat. For that she felt embarrassment and guilt.

He'd saved her life, but that also meant he'd been with her when she'd lost her baby. He'd seen her raw and exposed.

But he'd been kind. He'd also been professional and that was the way their relationship needed to go forward.

She'd written him a polite note, apologising once again for the slap and thanking him for his medical intervention.

During the last couple of months, she'd occasionally found herself thinking about him. His concern at the wedding, so harshly rewarded by her over-the-top reaction. His skill and his kindness when she'd lost her baby.

The feel of his hand…

Yeah, and that was entirely unprofessional. Professional was what she needed to be.

Moving on… The new, professional Addie.

She unlocked the door to the doctors' quarters and tugged her crimson, sparkly wheelie suitcase inside. Tugged? Not so much. This beauty wheeled at a touch. She let it go and watched in satisfaction as it freewheeled half-way across the sitting room. Nice. Her luggage was part of her new look, her revamp, her declaration to the world that she was moving on. This community needed a dedicated obstetrician and that's what they'd get.

Albeit a sparkly one.

She hadn't gone completely sparkly. Just a touch. She was wearing a rainbow-coloured sun frock, cinched at the waist. She'd let her hair fly free. Her now silver-blonde hair was streaked with soft amethyst streaks. She was wearing oversized amethyst earrings and a single drop necklace, and her brand-new glasses had a hint of amethyst in their silver rims.

She checked herself in the mirror above the hallstand and was pleased to approve.

And then she saw Noah. The fly in her ointment. This place was home…but Noah? A ghost from her past?

Her intention to stay completely professional flew out the window. Memories of that appalling wedding… Memories of her loss…

He'd signed on for six months. That meant he was here for four more months.

Maybe it was time she got herself her own place to live. The convenience of being right at the hospital for obstetric emergencies had kept her here, but there were alternatives.

'Addie...' He was dressed in chinos and a short-sleeved shirt, with a stethoscope dangling from his side pocket. He looked vaguely rumpled, as if he'd had a long day.

Tuesday was a normal day for scheduled surgery, she remembered. He'd probably have kept that routine, and such a day was often hard for a surgeon. Schedules didn't take into account unscheduled stuff that happened in a town like this.

'Hi,' she managed, trying not to think he looked tired. Or...gorgeous? How inappropriate was that?

'Welcome back.'

'Thank you. I'm pleased to be back.' She sounded absurdly formal. They both did.

'You look...well.'

So much for all the money she'd spent on her transformation. *Well?* But, then, what did she expect?

While she'd been convalescing she'd been in

touch with a couple of friends from back in Sydney. Noah's name had…just happened… to come up. Apparently there'd been a vitriolic end to his marriage. Was that why Noah had turned his back on his ascendant career to come to Currawong? Loss? Grief?

She thought fleetingly of Noah's wife. Ex-wife? Even in a wheelchair Rebecca had looked stunning. In comparison, *well* was as good as Addie could expect.

'I am well,' she managed.

'Can I give you a hand with your luggage?'

At least here was safe ground. 'No need,' she said airily. She walked across the room, turned the suitcase until it was facing her bedroom door and kicked it again. A little too hard and a little off course. It zoomed across the polished boards, slammed into the bookcase and a vase toppled off and smashed onto the floor.

Silence.

'I never liked that vase anyway,' Addie said at last, looking down at the mess of broken crockery.

'Designer ware,' Noah agreed. 'Supplied by

Bland R Us. I'm sure we can find something less sterile in Theatre.'

'Maybe a bedpan with cactus planted inside...'

'It'd have more personality,' he agreed, and she came close to a chuckle. And then she took a deep breath. The time had come. The time was now. 'I have a confession.'

'A confession?'

'I... We may have to put away...some stuff.' She looked down at the floor rug and grimaced. 'Like this. This has to go.'

'I can understand the vase getting in the way of your luggage,' he said cautiously. 'But...the rug?'

'I'm afraid it'll get eaten.'

More silence. And then... 'Uh-oh,' Noah said.

'I know I should have asked you.' She was talking too fast, her tongue tripping over the words. 'I know the lease says no pets and I thought...well, to be honest, I knew if I rang the hospital board and asked they'd say no— Morvena will have a fit!—but if I presented them with a *fait accompli* then they'll have to wear it. They haven't found anyone to replace me, have they?'

'Locums,' he said, frowning. 'They're not trying to replace you.'

'I doubt they can.' She said it with satisfaction. 'The good thing about working in such a remote area is they need to put up with who they can get.'

'Like me,' Noah said, and Addie cast him a suspicious look. If she didn't know better she'd think she heard laughter.

Actually, there might be laughter. Noah McPherson was way over-qualified for the job here. That Currawong Bay had his services for six months was amazing.

Six months.

Four more months of sharing a house...

'What have you done?' And there was no mistaking the laughter now. Those deep grey eyes were twinkling straight at her. She couldn't help responding. She smiled back and suddenly she felt as she had when she'd walked from the hair salon with her hair coloured. Like the world was opening up before her. With colour?

Well, that was dumb. There was no way Noah McPherson should have that effect on anyone.

'You'll have to see.' She crossed to her bed-room door and pushed her badly behaved suit-case inside.

'You have something that can eat mats in your suitcase?'

'I... No.' She kicked off her high heels be-cause, okay, she'd made a statement and she was home now. It was time to move on to the next thing. But she was home...with Noah?

Daisy would help. Hopefully. Nothing like a Daisy to ease tension. 'You want to see?' she asked.

'I want to see.'

'Okay,' she said, striving to sound nonchalant and not anxious at all. 'Let's go meet Daisy.'

Daisy was quite possibly the cutest golden re-triever puppy Noah had ever seen.

Addie had obviously decided to unpack be-fore introducing Daisy to her new home. Daisy was therefore currently tied to a veranda post surrounded by dog bed, dog bowls, dog toys...

And oldies.

The veranda was the preferred snoozing place for the residents of the nursing-home section of the hospital. It overlooked the sea and was protected from the prevailing winds. The big wicker chairs were usually filled with snoozers, soaking up the warmth of late summer.

No one was snoozing now. There was a cluster of oldies surrounding a pint-sized bundle of pup.

Was there anything cuter than a golden retriever puppy? Noah didn't think so, and Daisy wasn't about to change his mind. She looked about ten or twelve weeks old, and she was wriggling all over. Still tied to her veranda post—the oldies obviously hadn't ventured to untie her, although they were clearly longing to—she was tugging to the length of her leash so she could wiggle and lick and greet as many new friends as fitted into her orbit.

His first thought? Sophie would love this puppy.

No. He shoved the thought away, hard. Four months to wait…

'Oh!' Addie was sounding dismayed as she hurried forward toward the clustered oldies. 'I didn't mean to disturb you. You guys are supposed to be asleep.'

They weren't asleep now. Without exception, the residents of the nursing home had migrated to the doctors' house end of the veranda. Bill Harrison, ex farmer, was crouched on the ground, enticing Daisy to crawl onto knees that had been destroyed by eighty years of heaving hay bales. But it was doubtful if he was even feeling his knees. He was intent on unclipping Daisy's leash and his attention was on the pup.

'There's all the sleep in the world where I'm headed,' he growled now. 'Bugger naps. Where'd you get this one, Addie? She's a beauty.'

'She is, isn't she?' Addie beamed and plonked herself down on her knees with Bill. 'I've only had her since this morning. I picked her up on the way home, from a breeder in Sydney. I shouldn't have her here, but I thought you guys might be able to help look after her.'

'Us?' It was Ruby May Alderstone, a long-retired schoolteacher, shrivelled from years of rheumatoid arthritis and usually grim from constant pain. But now she was smiling, stooping from her wheelchair to click her fingers to entice Daisy to come to her.

'Only if you want,' Addie said.

Daisy launched herself from Bill's knees to Addie's, reached up and licked, throat to forehead, a great, slurpy dog kiss, and Addie giggled and held.

And Noah thought, I know why she's bought this dog.

He still didn't have a handle on Addie Blair. He'd worked with her occasionally back in Sydney when she'd been a newly qualified obstetrician, engaged to be married to one of his surgical colleagues. He'd thought her plain, mousy, competent. The couple of times she'd been in Theatre with him she hadn't joined in the general theatre banter. He'd thought her... boring. The fact that she had been engaged to Gavin had cemented that thought.

Then he'd seen her at what was supposed to be her wedding. She'd been beautiful that day, but beautiful in a strange way. It was as if she'd been dressed by others, transformed into a Barbie-type caricature of the real Addie. The boring Addie had still been underneath.

Then she'd slapped him and he'd seen fire behind the bland exterior. For the first time he'd seen spirit.

That spirit had seemed extinguished two months ago—and why wouldn't it have been? The Addie he'd seen in the hospital bed had seemed like she'd had the life snuffed out of her. He'd felt desperately sorry for her, but there'd been nothing he could do.

But now...she'd done something for herself. Not something. Some things. She'd come back perky and fresh and defiant. Her outfit was a far cry from the sensible Addie he'd first met, but it hadn't taken her back to the Barbie Addie of her wedding day. Her clothes, her accessories looked like they'd been chosen with care, and chosen...for fun? Her sun dress was fun and flirty. Her hair looked great.

She hadn't abandoned her glasses, as she'd done for the wedding, but she'd changed them for slightly oversized ones, with silver rims and hints of colour.

She was cuddling the wriggling Daisy and she was laughing and he thought...

Physician, heal thyself?

And then she turned a little and he saw a glimpse of what was behind. She was holding Daisy as if she needed her.

The loss was still with her, then. Disguised, but bone deep.

'What is *that* doing here?'

He glanced along the veranda. Uh-oh. Morvena.

Morvena Harris was the nurse administrator of Currawong Hospital. She was well into her sixties but she showed no sign of retirement, or even slowing down. She ran the little hospital with ruthless efficiency, and, it had to be said, with skill. The staff reluctantly respected her. Patients might sometimes feel they were being bossed into recovering but recover they did.

If there was a medical need, Morvena pulled out all stops to make sure her patients lacked nothing, but there was the rub. *Her* patients. *Her* hospital. *Her* rules.

Noah had already had a run-in with her over visiting times. A young mum, a dairy farmer, had been in with appendicitis and the only time her husband had been able to bring his kids to visit had been after milking, late at night. Which was later than the rules stipulated.

'You can visit your wife, but the children can't come,' Morvena had decreed. 'You can't guarantee they won't be noisy.'

Noah had looked at their distress and put his foot down. Morvena still hadn't forgiven him.

It didn't make it any better that she was Henry's mother-in-law. The affable Henry was like putty in his bossy mother-in-law's hands. What Morvena wanted, Morvena usually got.

Now she was looking at Daisy as if she were a bad smell. A very bad smell. Then she glanced at Noah. He couldn't wipe the smile off his face fast enough, and her expression darkened. As if suspecting mass insubordination?

'Who brought that animal onto the premises?'

'She's mine.' Addie looked up at Morvena and smiled, but Noah could see the shakiness behind the smile. This was defiance but defiance could only go so far. 'Hi, Morvena. This is Daisy. She's going to live with me.'

'Not here, she's not,' Morvena decreed. 'Dogs shed. Allergies present a nightmare. You know the rules, Dr Blair.'

'I've already rung a couple of my young mums,' Addie told her. 'They've offered to organise a roster for runs during the day. She won't be a problem. We can keep her in the yard behind the doctors' house.'

'She can't live on hospital premises,' Morvena snapped. 'The doctors' accommodation is hospital property. End of story.'

'Then I'll find my own apartment.' She tilted her chin and Noah wondered how many run-ins Addie had had with Morvena in the past. A few, by the look of things. Morvena was looking at Addie with the same kind of belligerence Noah had thought was reserved for him.

But was there fear behind Addie's defiance? Fear that something else was to be snatched from her?

Something settled inside him, something hard and unassailable. There was little he could do for Addie, but he could do this.

'She shouldn't be confined to the doctors' house yard,' he said, and Morvena gave a surprised nod of satisfaction.

'I'm glad you agree. Now—'

'She needs to be out here.'

'What—?'

'Daisy's a companion dog,' he said, inexorably. 'Her place is with patients.'

He was watching the Daisy in question turn from Addie to Ruby. The ex-schoolteacher bent with difficulty so she could pat the soft little ears and Daisy responded by trying to turn a complete circle on the wheelchair footrest. She failed, fell sideways, lay for a stunned moment on the veranda and then looked up and around with what Noah swore was a grin. Like, That was what I meant to do all along. The circle around Daisy convulsed in laughter. A couple of nurses, further down the veranda and obviously on their break, edged up to see.

'A companion dog...' Morvena snorted. 'What nonsense. They have to be trained. That dog—'

'Was obviously bred to be a companion dog,' Noah said. 'And you must have read the literature, Morvena. The effect of a companion dog on depression and anxiety in long-term residents of nursing homes can't be understated. It's associated with increased social interaction, increased confidence, decreasing levels of isolation and, most of all, fun.'

'If we wanted a trained companion dog we'd have organised one,' she snapped back at him. 'A proper one. With a proper accredited owner.'

'And you'd pay for it how?'

There was the rub. This little hospital ran on a shoestring. It might be excellent and well equipped, but there was no money for extras.

'And you do realise our nursing home advertising brochure is misleading,' Noah went on, pushing his point hard, while Addie and the elderly residents watched in a certain amount of awe. 'The brochure clearly states that activities are organised morning and afternoon. Lorna comes every morning to organise excursions and games, but the afternoon, Morvena?'

'The brochure was printed years ago,' Morvena snapped.

'And it's still being given to potential residents. The people here could sue for false representation.'

There was a shocked hush. Everyone held their breath. Morvena was staring at Noah as if he had two heads. Such defiance was obviously unheard of in her reign.

Addie was staring at him, too, her eyes wide, looking…hornswoggled.

'Hey, we could, too.' That was Bert Nanbor, a Vietnam veteran who'd managed life without a leg until a farm accident two years back had seen him lose the other. 'I came in after reading that brochure and I've sat on this veranda bored stupid every afternoon since. And allergies…' He snorted. 'This is outside. There's plenty of fresh air to blow allergies away, and we all have our own rooms. Anyone with allergies doesn't need to share. But even then… Allergies… Never had 'em in my day. Anyone here got allergies?'

There was a chorus of rebuttal. The nurses up the back were hiding their mouths with their hands. Stifling giggles.

'And we'll help you train him, Doc,' Bert added, turning his attention to Addie. 'Almost everyone here comes from farms and we know dogs. Bill here used to train working dogs, didn't you, Bill? This little lass looks smart as paint. We could have her herding sheep in no time.' And then he grinned. 'Or herding Mrs Rowbotham's hens. It's time those hens learned discipline.'

Addie had been trying to keep a straight face but she lost it now. She chuckled—and Noah glanced across at her and thought... Wow.

The chuckle transformed her. It lit her within.

Had he ever heard her chuckle?

He thought back to the serious colleague he'd worked with before her failed wedding. She'd been sober, conscientious, seemingly almost bowed down by the responsibility of getting things right.

Gavin had told him of the death of her father, and of Gavin's own father. Apparently they'd been engineers, working on a major bridge construction together. The bridge had collapsed when she and Gavin had been toddlers. According to Gavin, he and Addie had then been practically raised together, their mothers united by common grief.

'That's why we're getting married,' Gavin had told him, in those last desperate moments of justification, before Gavin had disappeared and left him facing the failed wedding farce that had followed. 'Addie's mother has cancer. My mum's gutted and she needs me to do the right thing. This was meant to keep all of them happy.'

Yeah, right. Good one, Gavin.

He'd lost touch with Addie after the wedding. She'd quietly left the hospital and he'd been caught up in his own worries. But now… The Currawong hospital grapevine—which spread to Noah whether he willed it or not—was good, and Addie had been here for almost three years. But the grapevine didn't know why—or even how—she'd become pregnant. There was communal disgust that it hadn't guessed.

In that appalling few moments before surgery, she'd told him she'd used donated sperm. Why? Had the experience with Gavin turned her off men for life?

Conscientious. Boring.

Watching her now… Was there a different Addie underneath?

He turned his attention deliberately back to the pup. What business of his was Addie's life?

'You realise Mrs Rowbotham is the hospital

housekeeper and weekend cook,' she was saying, stifling chuckles as she tried to respond to Bert. 'Eggs from her chooks feed the hospital.'

'There's no reason why that'll change,' Bert said blithely. 'If I was their size and I had this pup on my tail, I might lay an egg myself.'

It was too much. Everyone laughed, and Addie's chuckle was glorious, a lovely, tinkling laugh that seemed...

To be setting something free?

'You still can't keep the dog,' Morvena snapped, sounding driven against the ropes. 'It's against the rules.'

Addie's face fell but Noah thought, No one's going to mess with that chuckle on my watch.

'Then the rules change,' he growled back. 'Or I send a brochure to the Board of Health and complain of misrepresentation. Our advertising offers activities each afternoon but the advertisement's misleading. Here's Dr Blair, offering the use of her puppy for free. We accept or I act.'

'You wouldn't dare...'

'The consequences being? You'll sack me?

Or Henry will sack me? I'm only here until my permanent replacement arrives in four months and there are lots of other places I can go. If you have a queue of surgeons waiting to take my place…'

'They sweated trying to find a locum for Addie, and they've had no responses trying to find a permanent surgeon.' Bert was obviously soaking in the drama. 'Currawong without a surgeon…geez, Morvena, you'd have to close the acute hospital and send everyone except us oldies to Sydney. All for a bit of fluff that never hurt anyone.'

But the fluff in question had been getting bored. He'd wandered along the veranda to greet the one person he hadn't met yet. Morvena. Morvena was wearing sensible pumps, with sensible laces. Tied in bows. Daisy spotted the bows, quivered, crouched—and pounced.

Morvena shrieked. She raised her foot to kick Daisy away but Noah was there before her, diving along the veranda almost before Morvena reacted. By the time her shoe was aimed, Noah had scooped up the recalcitrant pup and was heading back to dump it in Addie's arms.

'Requirement number one,' he said. 'There'll need to be a gated playpen where only those who don't mind being chewed enter. It'll need to be easily accessed by wheelchairs, though. Any of you guys any good at building?'

'I used to be,' Bert said reluctantly. 'Can't do much without legs.'

'Woodwork's something you should be doing if you're bored in the afternoons,' Morvena said, glaring at everyone. 'The men's shed. You know the local citizens' group set it up. It's full of tools and benches suitable for wheelchairs but you never use it.' She glared at Noah, defiantly. 'We have all sorts of occupational aids no one uses.'

'Then isn't it lucky Daisy's here to encourage us to use them?' Noah said blandly. 'Bert, do you reckon you could whip up some sort of a doggie playpen. Bill?'

'I used to enjoy woodwork.' It was Ruby May, interspersing hesitantly from her wheelchair. 'It's years since I held a hammer, but I bet I still can. If the men do the bits that need strength, I'd love to help.'

'Excellent,' Noah said, tucking Daisy under

one arm. 'Give me a list of what you need and I'll head down to the hardware store. I'm happy to cover costs.'

'There's no need,' Addie started, but he quelled her with a look. There was a need but the need wasn't purely Addie's and Daisy's. She saw it, too, and gave a faint smile. And to give her her due, so did Morvena.

'You do woodwork?' she demanded of Ruby May.

'All my life,' Ruby said simply. 'Mum taught me.'

'You never join in any of the activities.'

'Knitting with my arthritic fingers? Bingo?' Ruby snorted. 'Would you?'

'But the shed…'

'It's got a sign on it saying "Men's Shed",' Ruby told her. 'No one invited me there.'

'Well, we're inviting you,' Bert said roundly. 'The sign comes down. Isn't that right, guys? And I'm covering the costs of the wood. No, don't argue,' he told Addie as she made an instinctive protest. 'What use is money if I can't have fun?' He chuckled. 'Fun… There should be more of it. We can keep her, can't we, Morvena?'

'Oh, for heaven's sake...' But Morvena had been trounced and she finally had the grace to admit it. Her sigh resounded along the veranda. 'But it's a responsibility, Dr Blair. If anyone gets hurt, if there's any damage, it's your responsibility.'

'It's our responsibility,' Noah added. He smiled at Addie, and surprised...the glimmer of tears? That spoke of fragility. She wasn't completely recovered, then.

He felt a pang of something that should be concern for someone who'd been his patient—but it was more than that.

Concern for a colleague?

Possibly more than that, too. He was feeling an almost overwhelming urge to step forward and hug her, hold her tight, sandwich-squeeze her and her wriggling puppy until the look of strain around her eyes eased.

Instead he turned business-like. 'Addie, you take Daisy and introduce her to her new home,' he told her. 'Tell her the back bedroom's mine and if I find her under the covers then all bets are off. She'll be booted out to Bert's bedroom before you can say woof. Right, we need a list. Ruby May, if I grab a pen and paper, can you tell us what we need? I have time before evening ward rounds. As long as there's no emergency, I can fit in a trip to the local hardware store. Addie, can you be trusted to keep the monster under control until I get back?'

'I can do that,' she told him, and even though she was smiling there was still the glimmer of tears behind her eyes. 'Thank you. Thank you all.'

'And special thanks to Morvena,' Noah said, and grinned at Morvena and kept grinning until that dour lady was forced to give a tight smile in response. 'Addie, medically, you, me and Morvena, we're a force to be reckoned with. And Daisy, too. Our medical team has just been increased by one.'

Morvena gave a snort of disgust and turned on her heel. There was a ripple of laughter through the ranks but it was short-lived. The residents had a project and Noah could see each and every one of them figuring how they could play a part.

Excellent.

And Addie?

She was smiling, too, and that was even more excellent.

His fast trip to the hardware store turned out to be not so fast because Bert and Ruby May insisted on coming with him. He had an SUV with roof racks—he had a kayak he used in his spare time—so he could fit wheelchairs, plus elderly companions in crime and still have room to accommodate the extensive shopping list.

'How big is this playpen?' he demanded, astounded, as piles of timber were loaded onto his roof rack, but Ruby and Bert just chuckled. 'Leave it to us, Doc,' Bert told him. 'You fix people. We fix playpens.'

And the extra time was worth it, he decided as he unloaded the timber into the workshop and watched the residents' delight. It was even worth the fact that he had to push back his evening ward round, and then cope with a farmer's kid who'd got in the way of a cow with a mean kick.

By eleven that night he was exhausted but in a good way. The laughter, the enjoyment of Ruby May and Bert, the anticipation rippling through the nursing home were still making him smile. He headed back along the veranda to the doctors' accommodation, pushed open the door and there was something else to make him smile.

An advantage of living in the doctors' quarters was that cleaning was provided. Mrs Rowbotham came in every morning and bustled about, worrying about 'her doctors'. She religiously cleaned the fireplace, set the fire and tut-tutted when he hadn't used it.

Noah hardly did use it. The days were warm. Occasionally the nights got chilly but he tended to work late, eat dinner on the veranda and then crash. But the fire was being used now. Addie had piled cushions onto the rug and had nestled there with her pup. The main light was off, and her face was lit by the flicker of the fire's embers.

Daisy was curled in the crook of her arm. She looked—they both looked—supremely, completely at peace. Neither of them stirred as he came in. He stood for a moment looking down at them, watching Addie's face. She looked young and very vulnerable. She looked...beautiful.

She'd get cold if she stayed there as the fire died, he thought, trying to drag his thoughts back to practical. After all, she was his patient—or she had been. She wouldn't be his colleague until next Monday when she officially started work again. So...if she was his patient it was his duty to look after her.

Should he wake her? Steer her to bed?

He didn't have the heart. Instead he headed for the blanket box and fetched one of Mrs Rowbotham's stash of fluffy comforters. He pulled out the softest, a pile of pink angora, and carried it silently back to the pair beside the fire.

He stooped and spread it gently across them. Daisy stirred, wiggled her tail gently and then closed her eyes again, as much to say, Don't you dare disturb this, this is perfect.

It was indeed perfect. He tucked the rug in and stayed for a moment looking down at them.

Addie's eyes flickered open. Met his. Smiled. It was a smile that reflected Daisy's.

'Thank you,' she whispered, as he tucked her in, and he could tell she was still ninety percent asleep. Dreaming? And as if in a dream, her hand came up and her fingers touched his face, a feather touch, maybe to see if he was real?

'You are a very nice man, Noah McPherson. Has anyone ever told you that?'

There was no need to reply. Addie's eyes fluttered closed. Her hand sank and he tucked it under the rug.

She smiled in her sleep. He had an almost overwhelming urge to stoop and kiss her goodnight.

He did no such thing. Once upon a time Noah McPherson's heart had been open to beauty, to gentleness, to love. Now he stepped back and made a silent vow.

He'd given his heart once and it was still cracked wide open. Who was going down that road again?

Not him. He left the room and went to bed.

CHAPTER FOUR

ADDIE SPENT THE next few days catching up on work. The hospital had managed to get a locum while she'd been away but there'd been little follow-up with patients with long-term concerns. There were pap-smear reminders, follow-ups with gynae, making sure pre-term mums were up to date with what they needed. She settled into her office and worked methodically through her files.

Her life settled into some sort of order. With the addition of her puppy.

Daisy was like a battery-driven toy without an off switch. She woke at dawn, full on, tearing around the doctors' house, chewing socks, chair le, anything she could get her teeth i Addie did her regular lurch to save precious thing she was trying to

Ever ded to be allowed into

Noah's room, but even if Addie had allowed it, by dawn Noah was out. He'd kayak or maybe run. The first morning after her arrival, when she took Daisy outside, she saw him down on the beach. He was running hard, almost as if he was exorcising demons.

She wondered about him. She knew so little.

He'd been Gavin's boss. In truth she'd been surprised when Gav had asked him to be best man as they hadn't seemed close, but then Gav had been a bit of a loner. Or she'd thought he was. It turned out there'd been a whole other side...

Whatever, thinking about Noah...

She knew he'd been married. She'd known Rebecca, but where was his wife now? He was no longer wearing a ring but surely the grapevine would have known if she'd died. Rebecca had been in a wheelchair but that was down to being injured in a past car accident. Nothing presently life-threatening.

So where was she now? It wasn't the sort of question she could easily ask. *Excuse me, but what have you done with your wife?*

And it was none of her business.

Their routine settled. Every morning Addie played with the pup in the back yard. By the time Noah returned from his run, Daisy was tiring. Noah sat at the kitchen table and ate cereal while Daisy snuggled onto his knee.

And every morning Addie thought... A guy who'd just run... Who'd showered and was still damp but looked...who looked...

Yeah, there was a route she wasn't taking. *He* was none of her business.

After breakfast she scooped Daisy up and headed over to the hospital. Daisy slept in her office, and when she woke she'd let her out onto the veranda.

There was 'stuff' happening on the veranda. The oldies were building a 'playpen', with wide gates and a ramp down from the veranda with wheelchair access. They were wrangling Daisy as they worked. Until the playpen was built Daisy still needed to be on a leash but they were having fun, being busy, being happy...

Sometimes Noah was out there, in breaks in his surgery, popping out to check that all was well.

To be happy, too?

It might be none of her business but the questions still came at her. Why was he here? A six-month locum while he got his divorce sorted? There were much more challenging jobs he could be doing, in any of Australia's cities. Why spend six months in such an out-of-the-way place as here?

Was he running, like she was? She'd come here after her wedding had gone wrong, after her mother's death. She'd wanted to run from everything that had reminded her of pain.

As the days passed, she found her thoughts drifting back to that time pre-wedding. To Noah.

It was no crime to wonder, she decided.

She thought back to the woman who'd been Noah's wife. She'd met Rebecca, both in her role as part-time receptionist at Sydney Central, and then at a couple of pre-wedding functions Gavin had arranged. Her impression had been that she was beautiful, opinionated and selfish, often seeming ready to manipulate her situation in order to get what she wanted.

Rebecca had summed *her* up in a glance and had made it clear what she thought of the ordinary little woman who'd made medicine her life. Being a surgeon's wife was much more important, Rebecca's attitude implied. Addie thought Rebecca herself had seemed bored—and often patronising to the man who'd been her husband.

For the life of her Addie couldn't see why Noah would be heartbroken at leaving such a marriage.

But that was her judgement, and her judgement only. Who could see what really happened inside a marriage?

And now...

Noah seemed a man in charge of his world, a man who had everything. But looking at him out on the veranda, watching him play with Daisy, helping the oldies put a gate into position...

There were shadows.

The shallow Rebecca must have had something she could only guess at.

Yeah, like sexiness and beauty and the ability to put people like her in her place, Addie thought, and tried to turn her attention back to her patient files.

But her attention kept straying to the man outside.

To Noah.

To none of her business?

Addie had brought the hospital to life, Noah thought as the week went on—and it wasn't just her puppy.

While she'd been away, he'd been aware that she'd been missed, that there was genuine affection for her. Now... Watching her move through the hospital, taking time to talk to everyone who'd like to talk, including those who weren't her patients, it was as if the hospital had regained something precious. Something good had returned.

With benefits, for Daisy was definitely a benefit. The pup was being snuck into the wards to visit those who couldn't get onto the veranda, and Noah could pretty much guess where Addie and Daisy were by the laughter that echoed down the corridors.

On Friday night he met her coming out of the room of Edith Oddie, an elderly woman he'd operated on for oesophageal obstruction.

Cancer was killing her fast. Noah had managed to clear the obstruction, but secondaries were appearing everywhere. For the last few days she'd been almost comatose, but as Addie emerged from her room with a suspiciously wiggly mound under an oversized cardigan, Noah was astounded to hear a crackly wheeze of laughter from the room she'd just left.

He stopped short and Addie looked up at him with a guilty grin. 'Not guilty, your honour,' she said before he could say a word.

'So you're not carrying a puppy under that cardigan?'

She gave a whirl like a three-year-old in a party dress, and the oversized cardigan flared out around her. It had moth holes in the hem.

'Three bucks from the welfare shop,' she told him. 'You like it?'

'Very nice. Moth holes being the new black. And bumps that wriggle…this season's latest accessory?'

'You guessed it.'

'Morvena would have kittens if she saw…'

'I bet she wouldn't. Kittens… *Ew*, allergies! And saw what?' she asked, all innocence.

'That I've decided bumps and moth holes are the new me?'

'I thought you'd decided on a whole new you when you came back here.'

Her face fell a bit. 'That obvious, huh?'

'Everyone's talking about it. Addie of the makeover.'

'I had to do something to cheer me up.' She sounded defensive. The bump wriggled under her breast and she heaved it closer. 'A makeover and Daisy. What else does a girl need?'

A baby, Noah thought, but he didn't say it. It hung, though, between the two of them.

'Don't look like that,' she said at last. 'I'm okay.'

'I know you're okay.' He smiled, pushing back an almost overwhelming urge to reach out and touch her. He didn't, though. Instead he motioned to the door behind them. 'Edith just laughed.'

'And so did her kids and grandkids.' She grimaced. 'They're a lovely family. I'm glad I got back before...' She hesitated. 'It'll be soon, won't it?'

'A couple of days.'

'Brian will be heartbroken. Do you know they've been married for fifty years? Fifty!' She shrugged and made a visible effort to put away the greyness that went with the profession. 'Me, I couldn't even manage a day.'

'I managed almost five before the divorce,' he told her, trying to match her insouciance, but he obviously failed. Her face creased in sympathy.

'I'm sorry. About you and Rebecca.'

'Don't be.' The words came out harsh but there was no way he could stop it. 'We should never...' He stopped, appalled at what he'd said. This was personal.

But Addie didn't appear to notice—or maybe she did. Her non-pup-wrangling hand came out and touched his arm.

'There's isn't such a thing as *should never* where love's concerned,' she said gently. 'I read that somewhere. You just...do.' Then she stepped away, blushing, as if the words she'd spoken had been far too personal. 'Like me and Daisy,' she managed. 'Love at first sight.'

'And like you and Gavin?'

'Love at first sight? That would have been

when I was two.' She peeped a smile that told him she was indeed over Gavin. 'My judgement may not have been completely formed. My mother tells me he nobly offered to share his lolly and I was smitten.'

'A true hero,' Noah agreed.

'And you and Rebecca?'

'I was driving a sports car.' He tried to make it sound like a joke. The words sounded hollow but she smiled.

'She fell for your car?'

'Like you fell for a lollipop.'

'Lollipop versus sports car. That must explain the difference in the lengths of our marital harmony.' They were both heading back to the doctors' house. She tucked her arm conspiratorially into his, which felt a bit inappropriate— until he saw Morvena bearing down on them. Then he understood. The contact allowed their combined arms to disguise the bump.

Blessedly Daisy didn't wriggle. Morvena passed with a cursory 'Goodnight' and the danger was past.

But then… Her arm was still in his. He didn't remove it. Why should he? It felt… It felt…

'I have a favour to ask,' she said, and he forced his thoughts from the direction he most definitely didn't wish them to go, and tried to focus.

'Yes?' he said, with caution.

'And that,' she said with asperity, 'is the tone of a colleague expecting to be landed with a ward full of patients while I swan off for the weekend. Which isn't true. I'm not swanning off anywhere. But, Noah...'

'But...' He couldn't help it. He still sounded cautious.

'I know this sounds daft.' Her voice had suddenly lost all confidence. 'And maybe it is daft. But you said...you emailed me when I was away and asked...'

And he knew. 'I asked you what you wanted for your baby.' He was with her now, understanding the hesitation. And the need for touch?

'I... It was good of you. I know most hospitals...'

'Most hospitals ask, if they can.' Embryos at the stage of Addie's pregnancy were so small there was often nothing to retrieve. But there had been something, and he'd made sure it hadn't been discarded from Pathology—that it had been kept until she'd made her choice.

'I said if it was possible…'

'It was possible,' he told her. 'That's why I emailed.'

'I know. And thank you.' Her voice broke a little but she forged on. 'You found out. You said she could be buried in the section of the cemetery or that you could organise for a cremation. And I said, yes, please to cremation, and Mr Rowlins brought the ashes to me this morning. In a tiny box with a rose carved into the lid. Which I gather you organised? He said you paid, and of course I'll pay you back. I'm so grateful.'

'You don't need to be grateful and you don't need to pay.'

'I do,' she said, firmly now. 'But now… I know it's an imposition but I wondered… Noah, there's a place where Currawong Creek meets the bay. I used to sit there and talk to her when I first found out that I was pregnant. I want her ashes there. And I thought… I wondered…'

'You wondered if I'd like to come with you?' And he got that, too.

Most people at funerals held onto someone. Most people needed someone.

But why had she asked him?

'Addie, there's no one else?' he queried. She'd lived here for almost three years. She had so many friends. Family? He knew her mother had died. He'd never heard of anyone else but, then, he hardly knew this woman.

'You were there for me,' she said simply. 'And you tried.' She gave a tired smile. 'And, yes, I have friends but they might…they might cry and I don't think I'm up to crying. Not any more.'

He understood. She needed someone to make the emptiness less…empty, but she didn't need to share her emotion. Well, he was good at that. Rebecca had been a world-class teacher. 'Let's do it,' he said simply. 'We can go there now if you like.'

'Now?'

'It's not sunset for another hour. I've finished work for the day. Would you like that, Addie?'

'I think so.' She took a deep breath. 'Yes. Yes, I would. Could you wait until I ask Heidi if she can look after Daisy for the evening?'

'We don't want her pouncing on ash,' Noah said gravely, and she managed a smile, oddly warmed by his humour.

'She would.'

'She definitely would. Shall I meet you in ten minutes on the veranda?'

'Yes, please. That would be...kind.'

Currawong Bay was a vast, sweeping spread of tidal flats, a sheen of sapphire water at high tide and a magnificent expanse of rock pools and glistening sand when the tide was low. It was a mecca for tourists, but mostly they gathered at the town end of the bay. If you want peace on a beach in Australia, walk a hundred yards from a car park, Noah thought as he and Addie walked silently along the path across the dunes. With so much beach space, few could be bothered walking further.

It had been a gorgeous day and the bay below the town was dotted with kids and mums and dads playing in the shallows, eating fish and chips, or simply savouring the beauty of the place. Five minutes' walk from the car park, the beach was much less populated. The odd dog walker was tossing sticks into the waves. Fishermen were setting up their lines for a night of hope.

Fifteen minutes' walk from the town there was no one.

Noah had run here during the last couple of months, using the space and peace of the place to try and come to terms with his interminable wait. He wasn't sure if it helped but it surely didn't harm, and he knew the path so well now that he was sure where Addie was going.

Sure enough, as the track veered right along the bluff she branched left, onto a rough, semi-overgrown path that ran along a trickling creek.

Two hundred yards from the beach the creek bed rose sharply, water rippling over rocks worn smooth by thousands of years. Then the bluff loomed above them and the creek became a waterfall, not so high, maybe fifteen feet or so. There was not much water at this time of the year but enough to form a constant, falling shower into a freshwater pool. Ferns hung lazily over the water and soft moss covered the rocks.

This was Addie's place? Noah had found this place, too.

'You know it,' Addie said on a note of discovery as they reached the water's edge, and he thought she must have read it in his face.

'It's part of my favourite run.'

'Which explains why the track isn't completely overgrown. I had to bush-bash my way in when I first found it.'

'It's worth bush-bashing,' he said, and she smiled. Like a co-conspirator. Someone who'd discovered that a little-known love was shared.

'I swim here,' she said. 'Whenever I can.'

'Me, too.'

'Skinny dipping?' Her smile grew wider.

'Why not? There's no one to see.'

'But now you know my secret. No skinny dipping for me for the next four months.'

'Four months?'

'Isn't that when you leave?'

'So it is.' Leaving was the least of it, but right now he didn't want to think about the end point. 'But no skinny dipping?' he asked, moving on fast. 'That'd be a shame. How about we agree to wear leper bells to warn each other we're coming.'

'I'm not sure you can buy leper bells any more,' she said cautiously.

'Sure you can. I'll put in a pharmacy request this very evening.'

'Can you imagine the reaction of the bureaucrats in Canberra when that rolls onto their database?' She grinned. 'You'll have the entire bay in quarantine before you can blink.'

'That might be interesting.'

'That might be chaos,' she said severely. 'We had enough trouble when Jason Kimber came home from overseas with measles.'

'Town shut down?'

'Almost,' she said. 'The mayor had a four-week-old son who hadn't been immunised, and the thought of measles was almost too much for him. It's a serious disease and we had containment organised fast, but our mayor was all for evacuation, which could have spread measles across all Australia. Can you imagine if we hinted at leprosy?'

'Maybe not, then,' he said gravely. 'Maybe just a cooee as we reach the last bend will have to be enough.' He glanced at the box in her hands and then at her face. 'Addie, do you want to do this alone? Would you like me to hold your hand while you say something? Stand beside you? Disappear for a bit?'

'I… No.'

'You want me to just shut up and…*be*?'

She gave him a shamefaced smile. 'You understand. Yes, please. Noah, I shouldn't have asked, but…'

'It's a privilege to be here,' he said simply.

He backed away, and settled on a rock a few feet back from her. Giving her space.

Letting her be.

It was time.

Except…it wasn't. Would it ever be time?

Addie stared down at the water. She felt the weight of the box in her hands and it was nothing compared to the grief in her heart.

It felt…overwhelming.

Noah had left her, not going far but far enough to give her privacy. She'd thought she wanted it but now…

The box in her hands... What it represented... Noah or not, she'd never felt so alone.

'I don't know that I can,' she whispered.

And she wasn't alone. Noah responded, his voice gentle, his words almost an echo of what was in her heart. 'Then you don't need to,' he said. 'Addie, there's no pressure to do anything at all. If you feel like you need to keep your daughter's ashes with you, then that's what you should do.'

'I need to let her go.'

'Then take your time. There's all the time in the world.'

'I want... Noah, I don't know what I want.'

She closed her eyes. She let her thoughts wander.

She talked.

'You know my father died when I was two?' she asked, maybe talking to Noah, maybe talking to herself.

'Gavin told me.'

'Did he tell you how dependent my mum was from them on? Over and over she told me, "If it wasn't for you, Addie, I'd kill myself." Fancy saying that to a child, but she did. "I want to be with your father," she'd say. Every time I disappointed her she'd say, "I'm only here because of you." I loved her and I'm sure she loved me but…no child should be raised with that sort of pressure.'

'They shouldn't,' Noah said, but still it was like an echo. He was asking no questions. Her thoughts could go where they willed.

She was gazing down at the waterlilies now, but she wasn't seeing them. She was seeing the barrenness of her past. She needed to talk about it.

What was it about this time, this place? This man? Why did she need to explain? She had no idea. She only knew the words were coming.

'So after the Gavin fiasco, after the pain of Mum's grief at our failed wedding, her illness, her death, I made a vow. I'd never depend on anyone like that. More, I'd never let anyone depend on me. Mum needed me to stay alive and that need almost crushed me. Then, when need was gone, it was like I was just…adrift.'

'And then?'

It was a question but a quiet one. If she

wanted to stop, right now, she sensed there'd be no pressure at all.

Strangely it made her want to keep going.

'I quit my job after…after the mess of the wedding,' she said. 'I guess you already know that. I think Mum was more gutted than I was. It was almost like she'd been holding the cancer at bay until the wedding, and she got sick fast. Then, after her death…'

She paused. Stared at the water again. Stared at the box.

'Don't tell me unless you want to,' Noah said gently.

'I do want to. Isn't that strange? You've been with me at two of the worst times of my life and now…it's like I don't have any secrets.'

'Addie…'

'I want to explain.' Was she talking to Noah? Somehow it didn't feel like it. She was standing by the water's edge, holding her box, talking or not talking to a man sitting on a rock behind her. A man she hardly knew.

It didn't make sense but the need to talk was almost overpowering.

'After Mum died I was struggling to come

to terms with who I was. I'd been so busy, so caught up in work, in care, in grief. And then, after Mum's death, there was nothing. And one morning I woke up and thought how wonderful would it be to love without…dependency?'

'Kids are pretty dependent,' Noah said wryly, and she managed a smile. But not at him. He was simply her sounding board, in the background.

'Yes, but not for ever,' she said. 'As a doctor I've seen so many mums with babies, toddlers, young children. I see total love—but there's more. Good parents, normal parents, they love their kids but even when they're tiny they're already launching them into their own lives. In so many ways they're teaching them to be free. And I can do that. Or… I thought I could.' She stared down at the little box and her grip tightened.

'So you decided to have a baby.'

'I did.' It was practically a whisper. 'But how? Dating left me cold. After Gavin… I thought I knew him so well. Would you go down that road again?'

'I guess not.' His tone was suddenly dry and

she had a flash of compunction. Rebecca… His wife…

'I'm sorry. I shouldn't…'

'Don't be sorry,' he said, roughly this time. 'Addie, this is about you. Tell me what happened.'

She turned and shot him a grateful look, but then went back to staring down into the water. 'I'm an obstetrician,' she said. 'I have friends who…well, the long and short of it was that I queue-jumped for sperm donation—but it didn't work.'

'Because?'

'Because of the endometriosis. At least, that's what they said.' She shrugged. 'So then I thought I'd get a job in the country, away from everything. I settled here and then decided to keep trying. Again and again. Finally I moved onto IVF. So many attempts. In the end I think I was just pig stubborn.'

'Because you wanted this baby so much.'

'I did.' She shrugged. 'And what's left? A tiny pile of ash, and it's time to let her go.'

Silence. He let her be while her thoughts drifted on.

'I can do this,' she said at last. 'I have a life. I have Currawong, a job I love, a community that needs me. I have an adorable dog called Daisy. I have a life where I'm not dependent on anyone and, apart from professionally, no one's dependent on me. I can be happy.'

'I'm sure you can be.'

'I just have to do this.'

'If you really want to.'

'This is what I want.'

'Then do it,' he said softly. 'Do it with love.'

He went back to being a silent, watchful sentry. Addie sat on the moss by the waterfall and gave herself a few moments of quiet. Of peace.

Of love?

A wood pigeon was cooing in the trees above her head, almost a lullaby. The water was trickling into the pool at her feet and a carpet of waterlilies wobbled in the faint current. She could see a fat, mottled frog on a lily pad, waiting for unsuspecting insects.

This was the right place.

The place to scatter her dreams?

Behind her Noah was now completely silent.

She shouldn't have asked him to come but she was now desperately glad that she had. As well as being with her, he was her link to the future, to her work, to Daisy, to the world she had to get back to.

And by letting her talk...he'd stopped the grey from descending. Who knew what could have happened if he hadn't been here? It'd be so easy to slip into the water with...

Um, not. That was her mother talking, not her. Besides, suiciding in three feet of water with frogs wasn't exactly an option.

She almost smiled. She almost turned and shared the thought with Noah.

Maybe not. It was enough that he was waiting to walk her home.

It was time to move on.

She shifted down the rock and unfastened the brass clasp on her box. The tiny container was beautiful, something she could keep and treasure. Had Noah guessed that? This wasn't a time to be thinking of Noah but she was still aware of his presence. It was something solid. Something to be trusted.

He seemed someone who somehow, weirdly, understood.

Her box was open now, revealing the tiny bag containing the ashes. She lifted the bag out and held it for a long moment. She thought... for ten weeks I was blessed. My daughter was real.

She waited until the heat from her hand warmed the ashes. It was all she could do. She let them go. They drifted slowly, settled, disappeared among the water lilies. The frog gave a gentle croak and leaped into the water. Ripples spread outward and then faded.

The evening's peace settled once again over the pool.

She was left with nothing.

She sat surrounded by bleakness, but suddenly Noah was there, slipping silently to sit beside her. He sat, his body just touching, shoulder to shoulder.

It was okay. She didn't want hugging or emotion, but the brushing of his body against hers was...necessary.

It grounded her. Gave her strength? Who

knew? It was a strange concept but the emptiness inside receded.

She turned to Noah and she smiled. 'Thank you, Noah. Time to go home?'

'Is this your home, Addie?'

She thought of this pool, of the beach, of the place she worked in, of the community who cared, of all the oldies caring for Daisy, of Mrs Rowbotham who bossed and worried her, of the nurses and other doctors who cared for her. Even the scary Morvena...

She turned back to the pool. The ashes had disappeared, absorbed into the life of this tranquil place.

'It is my home,' she whispered. 'I know it.' She caught herself. 'And how about you, Noah? Where's your home?'

A shadow crossed his face that she didn't understand, but he was pushing himself to his feet, giving her his hand so he could help her up, so she didn't slip on the moss. Gathering himself into himself?

'Who knows,' he said lightly. 'For four more months it's here. Home is just...where I am.'

That's not home at all, she thought, but she

couldn't say it. He was moving on. Getting ready to go.

Where?

The walk home was made in silence. Addie seemed lost in her own thoughts, and Noah…

There were so many thoughts in his head he had no hope of coming to terms with any of them.

He'd come here to support Addie. He'd left feeling shattered himself.

Too many memories…

Rebecca. His wife. A woman who'd been gutted because she couldn't get rid of a baby. A woman who treated a child as disposable—a child he was fighting for.

His lawyers had told him the chances of winning a court case were small. That he had to move on.

He couldn't without fighting, but if he lost, where was home then?

He couldn't think of it. If he didn't know where Sophie was…

Home was nowhere.

CHAPTER FIVE

IT SEEMED CHURLISH to get back to the hospital, say 'See you later' and leave it at that. But medicine had a way of filling spaces even when he didn't want them to be filled.

So Noah spent an hour suturing an eight-year-old's leg after a vicious dog bite. He spent another half an hour reassuring almost hysterical parents that he was sure their son wouldn't carry long-term scars—that was why the suturing had taken an hour. He then spent more time with council officers and police, making statements that would be used to deal with a dog that had been left to roam at will on the beach where the kid had been playing.

He fielded an aggressive call from the dog's owner, demanding that he change his statements, accusing him of blowing up 'mere scratches' into serious injuries.

He'd dealt with this kind of situation before

and he'd had Heidi take photographs every step of the way. He called the police again to keep them up to speed on the owner's aggression.

He checked in on Edith Oddie and found her slipping fast. 'But the puppy did her so much good,' her husband told him. 'Imagine…this afternoon she woke and she laughed. With all her girls here. I think…' He glanced at Edie's peaceful but unresponsive face. 'I think it's almost over but this afternoon she laughed…'

Tears were slipping down his face, but they were tears of acceptance, tears of peace.

Noah walked away and for some reason the conversation with Addie came back to him.

Fifty years married.

Some couples made it.

He walked back to the doctors' house and there was something heavy inside him. He thought of Edith's hand, held warmly, gently by her husband of so many years.

So much love…

He gave himself a mental shake. He didn't get emotionally involved. Or not more involved than he already was. There was no room. Four more months and he was out of here, no matter what happened. He pushed open the door of the doctors' house with decision—and decision was knocked out of him.

Addie had lit the fire and was sitting beside it, cuddling a sleepy Daisy.

'I know it's not cold,' she said, almost defensively, as he walked in. 'But the fire's good.'

'The fire's excellent.' He sounded cautious and he wasn't sure why.

'There's lasagne in the oven. Mrs Rowbotham left it. I heated it all so it might have dried out a bit. Sorry.' She waved a glass at him. 'But there's wine and you're welcome to share my fire.'

He hesitated. The night...the fire...the woman... The scene he'd just come from. This was intimacy he wasn't sure how to handle.

Addie...

Why had he been asked to share what had been such a personal moment this afternoon? He'd thought it was because he was separate—because she knew he wouldn't let emotion hold sway. It was an entirely reasonable explanation but now, looking down at her, he wasn't so sure that emotion could be contained.

Oh, for... This was ridiculous. She was a colleague. She'd asked him for a favour and now she was asking him to share her fire while he ate lasagne. And drank wine.

Maybe wine wasn't such a good idea.

But that was crazy, too. He was off duty as of now. One of the family doctors was on call tonight. He'd been inundated while Addie had been away and he'd had to make rules to give him time off. From Friday night, only the most dire emergencies saw him being called.

He could have a glass of wine.

So why was he hesitating?

He wasn't. It'd be dumb.

So he organised his meal, then settled in the armchair by the fire. Addie handed him a glass of wine and settled again, lying by the fire with her puppy.

'Thank you for today.'

'I don't need thanks,' he said brusquely. 'It was a privilege.'

There was silence while he ate, while he took his plate back to the kitchen, while he thought about whether he should leave her to her fire and her puppy and go to bed.

He came back to the fire, looked at the armchair and looked at the cushions on the rug, and then, as if he was someone he hardly knew, he slipped down onto the floor beside her.

Dumb? Of course it was but the scene was like a siren's song, infinitely enticing.

This woman was a colleague. He had no wish to get close. He had no wish to get close to any woman, but this evening there'd been grief and there'd been courage, and it seemed wrong to end it with a curt goodnight and leave her to her thoughts.

To her loneliness or his?

Whatever, he slipped down beside her, settled, refilled his wine glass, and stroked a puppy ear himself. Sleeping puppies were excellent for soothing all sorts of things. Daisy had obviously had a wild time with Heidi and Heidi's dogs. Right now, in sleep, she was giving Addie comfort.

She was curled on Addie's knee. He stroked her soft ear and it almost seemed like…

Um, not. If he couldn't get his mind away from that, then he needed to back away fast.

He stopped stroking Daisy and pushed himself back a little. He should retreat to the armchair, but he'd only just sat down and she might think...

What he was thinking?

What he had no business thinking.

There was silence for a while, broken only by the crackle of the flames. Things seemed to settle. Deepen? Become...something he didn't understand?

'Will you try for another baby?' he heard himself say, and then thought, Whoa, you have no business asking that. But she was gazing at the flames, fondling the ears of her sleeping puppy with one hand, holding her wine glass with the other, and it was almost as if the question was an extension of the night. A night where boundaries had been set aside?

Grief did that.

He thought of her face as she'd let the ashes drift into the water and he thought of his daughter. She hadn't been wanted but she was wanted now. Sophie.

She was not his.

And suddenly she wasn't looking at the flames.

'Noah? What's wrong?'

'I...' He shook himself. 'Nothing. I asked...'

'You did ask.' But she was still watching him, her attention deflected from the flames. From her own circumstances. She hesitated and he knew there were other questions.

Questions he didn't want to face himself.

'I don't know about trying again,' she told him at last, but she was still watchful. 'With my endometritis and after the IVF thing... It took so many trips to Sydney, so many failed attempts. I wanted it so much but then what happened...'

'It shouldn't happen again.'

'You don't know that, and the endometritis is still there. My chances of conceiving again... It took over two years. I'm not sure if I could bear it.'

'You're a strong woman, Addie Blair.'

'Strength only carries you so far. And honestly? I think strength is an illusion. People say you're strong because you don't crumble, but sometimes that feels almost dishonest. Because you crumble inside.'

'Is that how you feel now?'

'Like my insides are filled with something

that's shattered? It's how I felt two months ago. I've hauled it together, glued it back in place but it's like broken china. What do they say? "That which doesn't kill us makes us stronger?" I don't think so. It just makes us better at gluing up the cracks. The damage is still there.'

'And it hurts.'

'It hurts,' she said softly. 'So, no, I doubt I have the courage to try again.' She stooped and buried her face briefly in her puppy's soft fur. 'Daisy's it. Me and Daisy and the world.'

And then she raised her face and met his gaze full on. And something changed.

This was no longer about her, her gaze said. Her gaze locked to his, firm, kind yet inexorable.

'And now,' she said softly, but her tone said there was to be no quarter given. 'What about you?'

'What about me?'

'You get it,' she said softly. 'You get my grief over my baby in a way no one else does. Maybe that was why I asked you to come with me this afternoon. Yes, I knew you wouldn't break down on me or give me platitudes, but right from the moment of the ectopic diagnosis, I saw my grief reflected in you. And this afternoon… I watched my baby's ashes drifting away and I turned and saw you, and what I saw…' She shook her head. 'Noah, maybe it's not for me to ask but if you want to tell me…'

Did he want to tell her?

He hadn't told anyone. No one, apart from an explosion in his lawyer's office when grief and anger had built to eruption when the lawyer had read the last of Rebecca's demands. And her ultimatum.

He'd decided to stick it out, to fight, but his lawyers were telling him fighting had every chance of failing.

He had no choice. Useless or not, he had to try.

'You don't have to tell me,' Addie said. 'Only if you want to.' And then she reached over and took his wine glass, setting it and hers carefully on the hearth. As if clearing the path for whatever lay before them. 'Only if you can.'

'I don't talk about it.'

'Because you're a guy,' she said, wisely. 'Of

course. It's so much more manly to keep that stuff to yourself.'

'Like you telling everyone you were having IVF...'

She conceded, giving a rueful smile. 'Touché.' She hesitated again. 'But I have told you now,' she said. 'And it helped. It...helps.'

Yeah, but he didn't talk. Since when had talking solved anything? And Rebecca's threats still hung over his head. But she was watching him, waiting. She was...trusting?

The firelight was flickering on her face. The warmth, the wine...

This woman...

The barriers of years slipped a little and he didn't reach for them and shore them up.

Could he trust, too?

'Rebecca and I...we weren't a great match,' he said, and for a while he didn't say anything else. And neither did she. She simply sat. Just letting the night—and the trust?—settle.

The urge to talk was almost overwhelming.

Why? In five long years he'd never spoken but tonight...things had changed.

He talked.

* * *

'Rebecca was…well, you've met her,' he said. 'When she's at her best she's almost irresistible.'

'Yeah?'

He flashed her a look, saw the hint of laughter and smiled back. 'Okay, that was man-speak,' he said. 'But, believe me, she was, and I was ripe for irresistible. From the time I started med school I had my head in my work. I took big student loans, I worked nights to cover costs. I had a couple of relationships but they fell by the wayside fast. Even after I qualified as a general surgeon, I didn't stop driving myself. I was so damned ambitious. I headed to the UK for further training and then applied for the job at Sydney Central. That involved responsibility as well as skill and I was stressed. The first day on the job I met Beck.'

'I've seen Rebecca at her most charming,' Addie said, and he caught the note of dryness. Rebecca would never have bothered to be charming to Addie.

So he had to explain. He sought for the right words, words he barely understood himself.

'She can be lovely,' he said. 'But lovely's all on the outside. I was still caught up in the sheer effort of work, relieved that I was home and settled, but stressed by the responsibility of my new job. Beck was bubbly, effervescent, fun, and very, very beautiful, and I'd had my head in my work for so long it was like emerging into another world.

'I was too dumb to see it was financial security and the prestige of my job that she wanted. Given time, surely I would have realised, but I never had time. We were only a few weeks into dating when she was injured.'

He paused. He should stop now, he thought.

'So…do you want to tell me what happened?' she asked, and stopping wasn't an option.

'I crashed the car.' He closed his eyes, remembering the nightmare. 'We'd gone out to dinner with a couple of my new colleagues. She'd behaved beautifully but as soon as we were in the car she changed. The night had been boring, she said, so now it was her turn. She wanted to go on to a nightclub. It was one in the morning and I was on duty at eight. I refused and she kicked up a fuss. A real fuss.

Beck having a tantrum… I thought it was just the wine—she was certainly tipsy—but it was the real Rebecca showing through. It was quite a show and in the end she tried to slap me.'

'Story of your life, women trying to hit you,' Addie murmured.

He paused and he even found himself smiling. The pressure eased still further. He could tell her—but the smile disappeared.

'So I got distracted. It was raining, with sleet over the road. I cornered too fast, clipped the kerb and the car tipped. Beck hadn't fastened her seat belt and was thrown out.'

'Oh, Noah…'

The crackle of the fire helped as well, he thought. It was like a background of peace. This woman, this place, it seemed an oasis, as if the outside world was blocked out. It didn't seem as if he was exposing himself, his regrets, his anger. This was just… Addie.

'Paraplegia?' she queried. 'I don't know how complete. No one ever said…'

'And Rebecca never said either,' he said, remembering the shock, the diagnosis, the struggle to get her to attend rehab. 'She broke her spine at S4 but it was an incomplete break. When the swelling went down, feeling returned. Not completely but enough to make walking possible. By then. though, she'd cast herself firmly in the role of victim and she wasn't letting go. I know that sounds harsh, but it's true.

'Rehab was hard. The physios were asking her to do things that hurt and if there's one thing Rebecca won't do it's push herself anywhere it doesn't suit her. A month after the accident she'd remodelled herself. Doctor's girlfriend, damaged by stupid, careless doctor. Wheelchair bound. A woman who could spend her life being beautiful and making her man feel guilty. A woman who could make her man do exactly what she wanted.'

'Oh, Noah...'

'And she *could* walk,' he said, almost savagely. 'She can. If there's anything she wants badly enough she'll get it. Put a designer handbag just out of reach and she'll be on her feet and grasping. But no one's to know that.'

He shrugged, his face bleak. 'It doesn't matter, though. The truth is that she has suffered damage. The chances of her walking without a limp are remote and a woman with a limp doesn't suit Beck's desired image. Not enough sympathy. She loves her part-time job at Reception at Sydney Central, being the beautiful one in a wheelchair, three half-days of collecting gossip, vitriol, stuff she can use about anyone. The rest of the time…it's massages, beauticians, long lunches, making Rebecca beautiful for ever. And then…there's Sophie. Her little girl.'

He stopped, hearing the anger and bleakness in his voice, trying as he'd tried for so many years to hold it back.

'Sophie?' Addie said, obviously confused. 'Rebecca's child? I didn't know she had a child.'

'No one did,' he said flatly. 'But when Rebecca was in hospital, I was suddenly the one in charge.' He was talking to the flames now, caught in horror from years ago. He wanted to block it out, but for some reason he couldn't stop talking. 'Beck's alienated her family. They live in Canada but she moved on from them years ago. She has no one, so the hospital ended up putting me down as next of kin. Referring to me. While Beck was out of it with painkillers, they gave me her phone. I was using her contacts, trying to locate any friends or family who might care, when there was a call from Child Welfare. They needed to talk to her. They told me she had a twelve-month-old daughter. Sophie.'

'But there's never been any talk of a child.'

'That's because Beck simply cut her out of her existence,' he told her. 'From what I found out, two years before she met me she was going out with a guy with lots of money but no scruples. She thought pregnancy would force him to marry her, or at least give her whopping financial support. She got pregnant. She didn't bother with any of the tests because, well, why would she? This baby was simply a means to an end. But Sophie's father has even fewer morals than Rebecca. He disappeared overseas. It was too late to terminate the pregnancy and Sophie was born with Down's syndrome.'

'Oh, no!'

'And don't bother feeling sorry for Rebecca,' he said, roughly now. 'The Rebeccas of this world move on and move on fast. She wanted to get rid of it any way she could. Adoption was hard because she'd named the father on the birth certificate and no one could contact him. It involved hassle and Beck was never one to bother with hassle. So Sophie was placed in foster care. That's where I came in. The call was from Social Welfare saying Sophie's foster parents had a family drama and couldn't keep her. Rebecca was in and out of a drugged stupor and I felt responsible. So Rebecca emerged at last to have me by her bedside holding a beautiful, cherubic little girl, Sophie, a baby who twisted her way into my heart without even trying.'

'Oh, wow...'

'So then I copped a sob story,' he told her. 'How this guy, the baby's father, had fleeced Rebecca for everything she had. How she couldn't afford to keep her beautiful Sophie. And how much she was depending on me. And when Social Welfare moved in, asking questions, she simply clung to me and said, we'll be okay, we're a family, Noah's marrying me.'

'You didn't even propose?'

'I didn't have to. Come on, Addie, you know

the rules. Successful doctor smashes car, leaves his girlfriend in a wheelchair, a woman with a baby, a woman totally dependent. The car crash was my fault, Addie, and I accepted the consequences. And besides...' he gave a rueful smile '...I *had* fallen head over heels in love. But it was with Sophie.'

'Your little girl.'

'Except she wasn't.' The bleakness slammed back. 'The moment Beck came home from hospital she demanded Sophie go back into foster care. And to be honest I had to concede it was...almost sensible. Beck was struggling with rehab and the bills were mounting. I'd put myself through med school, then spent a fortune on further training overseas. I had debts up to my ears. I had to go back to work and I had to find somewhere suitable for Rebecca to live. I couldn't afford to pay for a carer for Beck, plus a carer for Sophie.

'So we agreed—temporarily—to use foster care. With access. But pretty soon I realised I was the only one caring about access. I brought Sophie home again and again, but Beck would have nothing to do with her. Once she'd used her to wedge me into marriage, she didn't want to know about her. She never talked about her. I wasn't permitted to talk about her. It was like she didn't exist.'

'Hell, Noah...'

'It was, and I should have walked long before I did. But I still felt responsible and there was now the overriding complication that if I walked I'd have no access to Sophie. Beck soon realised it, and held the threat over my head. And sometimes... The days when I collected Sophie, held her, played with her in the park...' He stopped and smiled, remembering. A hand tucked into his. A little face lighting up as she held up her arms to be picked up when he arrived to collect her.

'I couldn't leave,' he said, and it was all he could say.

'So what happened next?' she asked, slowly, cautiously.

'We lived like that until last year. A marriage that wasn't a marriage. Beck played her poor-little-me role to the outside world and I did what I needed to do to get by. Sophie's new foster parents turned out to be lovely. I was seeing her when I could, but burying everything else in my work. But then we were notified that Harold and Beth—her foster parents—had decided they were too old to continue. They were reluctantly relinquishing her at the end of the year, and Sophie would have to change foster parents—again. I was appalled, but Beck said, "So what?"'

He shook his head, trying to block the remembrance of that night, holding the letter, seeing Sophie being discarded yet again.

'I saw red,' he admitted. 'I told Beck that Sophie was coming home, like it or not. I wouldn't stay in the sham of a marriage if I couldn't care for her. And, as Beck's husband, as Sophie's stepfather, I was applying for legal adoption.'

'Good…good for you,' Addie said, a trifle unsteadily. 'I think.'

'Yeah, holding a gun to someone's head is such a good idea,' he said bleakly. 'Or not. We had the worst row but finally she agreed. Or I thought she'd agreed. She gave me details of Sophie's biological father and signed forms allowing the authorities to contact him. He signed the waivers. Everything looked like it was going ahead. When the adoption went through we'd bring her home. I told her if Beck wanted, we'd tell people she was my daughter, not Beck's. Or I'd say she had no former connection to either of us. Whatever Beck wanted. But obviously Beck didn't like it. Her agreement was just playing for time.'

Silence. Addie didn't comment. Her expression was carefully neutral. Too neutral. Was she feeling his pain?

Because pain was suddenly there, in spades.

He wanted to stop but he'd gone this far. He had to force himself to tell her the rest.

'After she signed the adoption papers she seemed...wired. I thought it was just the prospect of Sophie coming to live with us but obviously her worries went deeper. She refused to talk about Sophie being with us. She refused to let me bring her home until my application for formal adoption was approved, and with no authority I had to accept. So I threw myself into my work and waited. While Beck...thought of another way.'

'Another way?' It was a flat question, echoing bleakness. As if Addie knew what was coming?

'I was at a conference in Denver when she told me,' he said. 'By phone. She was drunk and laughing. Triumphant. Apparently she'd met… someone she describes as her perfect man. He's twenty years older than she is, wealthy beyond belief, someone who obviously loves the poor-little-me image. She told me she was filing for divorce. Irreconcilable differences. I can't fault her there.'

'Oh, Noah…'

'So when I got home I expected she'd have moved out. But she was still there, sitting at the kitchen bench, drinking wine. She'd just come from the beautician. She looked stunning. Beautiful. Smug. And she was waiting to tell me that she had all her ducks lined up in a row, and none of them included Sophie.'

He was hardly talking to Addie now. He was seeing the woman he'd cared for for so long. Looking at her smugness. Feeling the desolation of what she'd done in the past and was doing now.

'I walked in and she put her glass down on the bench, tilted her chin, arched those beautiful eyebrows and threw it at me. Her new man cared for her much better than I did. He had money but she wanted two-thirds of my assets. I'd done this to her legs and apparently I still owed her, big time. And, by the way, she'd notified Social Services that we'd split. The adoption was off.'

And that had been the thing that had gutted him. That still gutted him. He'd never felt such anger. Such helplessness.

'But if you still wanted it...' Addie whispered. 'Why wouldn't she let you proceed?'

He had to force himself to go on. To make himself say the words.

'She said Sophie was nothing to do with me. She was vitriolic, hissing hatred. But she said... I'd be her ex-husband and if I stayed in Sydney and adopted her, sometime in the future someone could figure it out. Did I think she wanted a mutant appearing from her past? And when I said I'd move, take Sophie to another city if she wanted, it was like a dam burst. The fury... She blamed me for her legs. She even blamed me for Sophie.'

'No...'

'She kept calling her a mutant. She said she

should have aborted her and it was my fault she was still saddled with threats of contact now. She wanted nothing to do with her and nothing to do with me. And I could no longer have access. Also I had to shut up. She knows how much I love Sophie and she has that covered. She has a second passport—Canadian. If I made a fuss she'd take her overseas and stage a breakdown. That's what she's done here, playing the foster system. She said she'd dump her on any foster system that'd have her, and she wouldn't even have to tell me. If I knew what's good for me, I'd shut up. Get myself a new life but don't mess with hers.'

Addie was watching him, her face telling him she was appalled. As well she might be. Why on earth had he shared? He'd suppressed his grief, shoving it on the back burner, using anger, coldness, action to move forward. Now it was exposed and he felt raw. He could read Addie's face and the feelings he had were reflected there.

'So that was that,' he said, bleakly now, like the past was something he couldn't escape from. 'I walked back out and I haven't seen her since. Neither have I seen Sophie.'

'So where is she?' Addie whispered. 'Where is she now?'

'She's still with the foster parents who love her. That's the one good thing but it's small comfort. After this mess, Harold and Beth agreed to keep fostering for twelve more months. They're wonderful but they're elderly. Harold's been diagnosed with a heart condition and any minute now Sophie will have to be moved. I've had access, played with her, loved her for five years…'

'Oh, Noah…'

'But I can't go near her,' he said, still bleakly. 'The next time I went… Beck said she'd put a block on my access. Even though she doesn't want her, she won't let me near. Legally I have no rights. But I've decided to fight. I don't have a choice. The social workers seem to be on my side, even though their hands are tied. I've consulted lawyers and reinstated my adoption application. The court hearing's in four months and I'll fight until every avenue's exhausted. Meanwhile, legally I can't go near her. That's why I'm here. I can't bear to be so close and not see her.'

'But I still don't understand. Why doesn't she want you to have access?'

'It's not logical. Maybe part of it's punishment, for someone who damaged her legs. More probably she thinks it'll get out. Sophie's existence has always been kept secret. It doesn't suit Beck's image to have deserted her daughter. I suspect her new man doesn't know about Sophie either. She'll never accept any promise I make. To Beck, promises mean nothing.'

'But you could tell anyway.'

'And let her take her who knows where? For revenge. She's perfectly capable of it.'

'Oh, Noah…'

He shrugged. 'So that's it,' he managed. 'I'll stay here until the court case. If I win I'll head back to Sydney. If I lose my application for adoption I'll still fight for access but if I don't get that… There's a neurology training programme in London that…might keep me busy. But I'm sorry I told you. Before the case comes to court Beck has complete control. Even now, telling anyone risks everything, and I had no right to land it on you.'

'Noah, you do have the right,' she whispered, and before he knew what she intended she leaned forward and took his face in her hands. 'Of course you do. Noah…'

She faltered as if looking for words, but there were no words. They both knew that.

The silence intensified. The fire crackled next to them. Daisy had slid off Addie's knees and onto the rug and Noah noticed. He noticed a tiny wrinkle between Addie's eyes, a crease of worry. She shouldn't worry. This was his grief. His…

'Noah, don't,' she whispered, and she leaned forward, just slightly, just enough.

And she drew his face to hers and she kissed him.

It was supposed to be a whisper kiss.

Actually, it wasn't supposed to be a kiss at all. She'd had no intention, no desire, no thought of kissing anyone, much less Noah, a colleague, a man who'd seen her at her most vulnerable.

A man she'd used for his strength.

A man who didn't need a kiss. Even a fleeting kiss. A kiss of comfort.

But this kiss was not of her making. It was an instinctive, almost primeval response to pain, and she'd moved before her head caught up with what her body was about to do.

What her mouth was about to do.

Her mouth intended to kiss him.

Even then the kiss should have been a brush of lips against cheek. She should never have aimed for his mouth. She surely didn't intend to.

But it happened.

Her mouth brushed his and his hands came up. In defence? To put her away? Who knew, because forces bigger than both of them seemed to be in play.

Instead of putting her away, his hands caught her face, his fingers cradled her cheeks—and the feather kiss became…

A kiss.

A kiss to change the world?

There was a stupid thing to think but somehow she was no longer thinking.

There was only this moment.

There was only Noah.

There was only need.

For in that one blinding moment, things changed. One moment they were by the fire, colleagues, maybe even friends, but a man and a woman who didn't know each other very well. A man and woman who'd experienced past pain and acknowledged each other's grief.

Addie was a woman who'd spent most of her life doing what was expected of her. Caring for her dependent mother. Carrying her mother's grief. Agreeing to marry a man she'd thought she trusted, a man who had been part of that expectation.

And Noah? He was a man who'd been in a bleak and loveless marriage, who'd been treated in the worst possible way.

Maybe there should be bleakness between them. Maybe this night should be one of reflected grief.

But there was no grief now. Not in this cocoon of firelight, of warmth, of wine.

Not in the touch of two mouths meeting, or in the way Noah's hands cupped her face.

Not in the way her body responded.

She needed…

Him?

She didn't know. She was beyond knowing. All she knew was that she needed this moment, she needed his touch.

She needed his body.

And he felt the same. She knew it as surely as night followed day. His kiss was deepening, deepening and she felt she was drowning in it.

And she wanted to drown. She wanted to sink into this man's body, to take what she needed from him, and to give what he needed from her. The loneliness, the grief, the bleakness of the last months, no, the last years, had somehow melted. For in this moment there was only Noah and his mouth on hers and his lovely hands drawing her closer.

'Addie…' His voice was a ragged whisper, and she could hear the desire in it. The naked need. 'Addie, we shouldn't. We…'

'We can.' Somehow she made herself answer. 'Noah, right now, we need each other.'

There seemed no room for more words, because something larger than either of them had taken over. Desire had built to a point where it couldn't be gainsaid.

Addie spent half her professional life dealing with the consequences of desire. She should have had far more sense than to let herself sink into this blissful abandonment.

But this wasn't sense. This wasn't even Addie. This was a moment out of frame, and she was suddenly a woman she hardly knew. She was the responsible one, the carer, but right now... to hell with consequences.

Daisy stirred and yawned, a great, goofy yawn, and it gave them pause. Noah broke away. He looked down at the pup in the fire-light and smiled. And such a smile...

It was tender, it was loving, it was all the things Addie most wanted, had dreamed of...

The smile was for the pup on the floor beside the fire. Of course it was. But it didn't matter.

And then he was gathering her into his arms, tightly, fiercely. Amazingly the smile was still there. For her?

And neither had to say what their intentions were. They knew.

'You're sure?' he whispered.

'I'm sure.' How could he ask?

'I haven't…hell, Addie, I don't even have condoms. I could… The pharmacy…'

Stopping now? Heading to a locked pharmacy and trying to find what they wanted?

And for what? If she wasn't so immersed in need she could have laughed. 'I have endometriosis and a history of impossibility of conceiving,' she managed. 'No luck with straight sperm donation. Two years with a petri dish. Plus I haven't even started my cycles yet. And yes, I know better. But surely…' Dear heaven, she wanted him so much. 'Surely we can risk…'

'We shouldn't.' But she heard it in his voice. He needed this moment—this night—as much as she did.

'I know we shouldn't,' she whispered. 'But we're consenting adults and…we can. Let's just, for once in our lives, be totally, absolutely irresponsible.'

He chuckled and with that the moment of defence—of sense?—slipped away. 'Let's,' he said.

And then there was only each other.

'Your bed or mine?' His voice was husky

with desire as he rose to his feet, with Addie somehow magically cradled in his arms.

'How about both?' she managed. 'One after the other?'

CHAPTER SIX

SHE WOKE IN the small hours to whimpering.

They were in Noah's bed. She was spooned against his body, cocooned in half-sleep, encased in pleasure. In happiness? Who knew, but it surely felt like it.

It was still dark outside and there was a puppy whimpering by the bed. Noah stirred and chuckled as he realised what the problem was. He kissed her gently, tenderly, meltingly, and then set her back from him.

'Needs must,' he murmured, and rose.

'Come back to me,' she heard herself say, and couldn't believe it was she who'd said it.

'Never doubt it.' She heard the smile in his voice, the smile that melted her heart, the smile she'd dissolved into.

And then he was gone, scooping up Daisy on the way out. She heard him open and close the refrigerator door. She heard him murmur to the pup.

She didn't stir.

Daisy was her puppy. Her responsibility. But right now responsibility was nowhere. This wasn't Addie the responsible, Addie the dutiful. This Addie felt almost wanton, outrageous… free.

What was it about this man?

It wasn't this man, she told herself. It was this moment. The circumstances. The moment was fleeting but she'd take it with both hands and hold on tight.

And then he was back, sliding down onto the sheets beside her, gloriously naked. His skin was against hers and it was the most magnificent feeling, erotic and wondrous.

He tugged her against him, chuckling into her ear.

'Sorted,' he said. 'Or…sort of.'

'Sort of?'

'We may have puddles to attend to later, but I decided they could wait.' His mouth started doing amazing things to her ear. 'Everything can wait. It has to.'

And she felt herself smile and the smile was huge. It seemed to envelop all of her. She turned so she was hard against him, her breasts crushed against his chest, her arms holding him. Her smile just seemed to grow wider.

'We have more urgent matters to attend to,' she managed, and proceeded to attend to them. With diligence. With laughter.

With love?

Morning happened, even when you willed it away with every fibre of your being.

Morning and reality.

She woke and she was still ensconced in the warmth, the incredible sensation of being one with this man, the feeling of his whole body cradling hers. It felt like she was on an island, a sanctuary, a place where time had stopped. There was only this man. She felt...

Loved? That word had crept into her heart in the small hours.

But it was morning. Time for reality.

And love? The word was enough to pull her out of her fantasy, to have her body stiffen, to have fear step in.

And he felt it. Of course he did. Was there any nuance this man didn't get? He was awake in an instant, drawing back, concerned.

'Addie...'

'What have we done?' she whispered.

'Acted like two teenagers without the benefit of sex ed classes?' He smiled, that gorgeous smile that did her head in. 'And now we're remembering what Mrs Nottle told us in Sixth Grade. Or Professor Clancy in First Year Med.'

'That you never, ever sleep with someone without the checks.' Despite herself, she was smiling. 'I'm not sure about you, but I had a Professor Yardman. She was insistent we head straight to the nearest clinic the moment we thought about holding hands and got ourselves tested for everything from dandruff to bubonic plague. And then we demand certification from at least three practicing medicos that our intended partner was free of the same things.'

'And then take all steps, up to and possibly including building brick walls, to prevent pregnancy.' His smile faded, concern overriding laughter. 'Addie...'

'I wouldn't worry.' She couldn't keep the trace of bitterness from her voice. 'The health stuff is okay from my side. I was checked within an inch of my life before IVF. And pregnancy? Fat chance of that.'

'Health is okay from my side, too,' he said, but his eyes were still worried. 'But, Addie...'

She got it. With his history... With Rebecca's betrayal... Of course he'd be gutted if anything happened. And they had been stupid.

'There's always the morning-after pill to make sure,' she told him. She sighed and tugged back a little more. 'We *were* dumb. We were needful.'

His hand rested on her waist and the feel of him... 'Addie, it was a great night. An amazing night. We could maybe...'

But reality was now crashing in from all sides. What had they been thinking? There were no maybes.

'We couldn't.' She knew what had to be said. 'Noah, don't even think about letting guilt push this further. We were both emotional. We drank wine when our senses were heightened. We took what we needed. And I did… I did need it, Noah. In truth, I loved it.' She sighed again. 'Confession. I've never had a one-night stand before but I know what it is. This. No strings attached. Moving on.' She managed to get her smile back in place. 'And you know what? It was amazing. Fabulous. Just what the doctor ordered. But it's over and I believe Daisy needs breakfast.'

'You really want to move on as if nothing's happened?'

'I… Yes.' But his hands were still on her waist.

'Addie?'

'Mmm.'

'I gave Daisy a snack at three a.m. She can wait a little longer for breakfast.'

'Noah?'

'Mmm.'

Say it, she thought. Say you don't want this.

But…maybe she could say it after she let herself dissolve in his body one last time?

How could she not?

A one-night stand should last at least until breakfast.

Medical imperatives were there even when you least wanted them. Two hours later the phone rang. A local farmer had rolled his farm bike and was on his way in with a crush injury. Cliff was already on his way to act as anaesthetist. Noah was needed.

He showered and disappeared. 'Sorry, love, to leave you with the puddles. What sort of irresponsible people leave puppies in the living room unattended?' He kissed her briefly, hard, and left in a hurry.

She was left with…regrets? Confusion?

Peace.

Mostly peace, she thought. Despite the lurch of sadness Noah's story had brought to her world, the night before seemed to have settled something deep within her. This wasn't a relationship that would go further. She knew that. Neither of them wanted it. But they'd been together in the right place, at the right time, giving comfort when comfort had been needed.

The age of comfort of loving.

Love? That word was still hovering.

It had been loving, she thought as she showered, much slower, much more languorously than Noah's fast ablutions. She had no urgent cases. She gave herself time to emerge from the night with peace.

Her world was waiting for her, her mums and babies, her ladies with gynae problems, the world as she knew it. But her world had changed.

Why?

Because she felt…

'Like a woman,' she whispered, soaping herself, feeling the warmth of the water slip over her skin, savouring the sensation of feeling like…

She'd been loved.

She wasn't in love. That was a crazy thing to think. After all, how well did she know the man? Hardly at all.

And yet he'd loved her.

Making love… She'd heard that phrase time and time again, often by teens, accidently pregnant. 'We only made love that one time, Doc. I never thought...'

She'd never thought either. That she could be so irresponsible. That she could sink so deeply, so fast.

Irresponsible...

She thought fleetingly of patients, the teenage girls she'd seen so many times in her career.

Pregnant.

'It was just the one time, Doc.'

Pregnant? It had taken four rounds of IVF before she'd conceived. The chances of pregnancy were...

Not nil. She'd told Noah she'd take the morning-after pill. It was only sensible to cover all bases, and now it was time she was sensible.

She dressed and made toast and coffee and took Daisy out onto the veranda. Daisy's friends weren't outside yet but she made the most of the space, haring along the veranda so fast she fell over her own feet. She attacked the doormat like it was the world's most vicious snake and it was her duty to kill it. She hared back to Addie and bounced, then raced off again as if to ask why she wasn't joining in. This morning was delicious. The world was waiting.

The trip to the pharmacy was waiting. The morning-after pill.

But Addie was having a conversation with herself.

It's dumb. I'll never be pregnant.

It's responsible. You know there's a slight chance...

'A chance.' She said the last two words out loud and Daisy bounced straight back to her as if she'd been called. Addie lifted her and hugged, hard.

Why was she hesitating?

Did she not want to take the pill? Did she not want to make sure?

Where was her head going? She couldn't handle any more useless hope. The grief of another failed pregnancy could well tear her apart. She'd decided—sensibly—to move on.

Hadn't she?

Maybe she hadn't moved far enough.

'This is nuts,' she said, and Daisy looked anxious. 'There's no decision to make. It doesn't matter if I take the pill or not. But…if by some chance it does matter, I don't want…'

She faltered. She didn't want…what? If by some miracle…

She let Daisy slip down to the ground, and unconsciously her hands moved to her belly.

What was she thinking?

What was she risking?

'My head's not working any more,' she told Daisy, but Daisy was distracted and no longer listening.

Addie stood and stared out to the horizon. There was a fishing boat, way off, almost too small to see.

Her hands held her belly tighter.

'I can't do it,' she said, softly now but with resolution. 'To risk…'

See, there was the problem. She didn't know what she was risking.

Disaster all over again?

This was crazy. She was overreacting, to say the least.

Noah would say she was overreacting.

Noah.

She glanced along to the far end of the veranda, to the Taj Mahal of puppy playpens built by the oldies—with Noah's help—and she knew what she had to do. At least she knew the first step. 'It's Saturday morning,' she told Daisy. 'I have stuff to do and I need to do it now, because staying in this house one more night with Noah McPherson is just plain dangerous. And I need to decide...'

She paused again. Regrouped. Figured it out.

'Okay, that's not fair,' she said to herself at last. 'There's been too much of *I singular* in Noah's life already. And in my life? This time, *we* need to make a decision. Go get the pill, Addie Blair, and then move on with your life.'

Saturday was busy. The weather was amazing. Locals and tourists alike were making the most of it and Noah was coping with the consequences.

Two kids collided in the surf with their boogie boards. One had a broken nose and fractured cheekbone, the other had a dislocated collar bone.

A dad showing off his new Oriental kite to his kids hadn't figured the power and strength of his new toy. The owl-like kite had done a nose dive and split the side of his face. All the young father could think of was his kids, though, so while Noah stitched his face he muttered over and over again, 'Thank God they weren't underneath. What was I thinking?'

He went away with his face bandaged, clutching his wife, clutching his kids, and Noah watched him go and thought...

Yeah, not a good thought. He'd moved on from that particular fantasy.

But he'd slept with Addie...

A thirty-year-old was brought in from the beach, a drunken jet-ski rider with the brains of a rather small newt. He'd tried to make his jet-ski jump over a sand bank and even the paramedics were shaking their heads over his idiocy. He had broken ribs and femur. Noah was having trouble trying to differentiate drunkenness from concussion. Anaesthesia for drunks was incredibly fraught, so he and Cliff were kept busy for what was left of the afternoon.

By the time he finished he was dead tired but he headed back to the doctors' house with a sense of anticipation. Fish and chips on the back step with Addie? It sounded good to him. If she wasn't doing anything…

She wasn't there.

He opened the door and no puppy launched itself across the room to meet him. There was no dog basket by the fire. Not a single puppy toy.

Addie's bedroom door was open. The bed was stripped, the blankets neatly folded. Her dresser was bare.

He walked slowly across and pushed the door wider.

Nothing. No clothes. No personal belongings. No bright, shiny suitcase.

The room was stripped as if she'd never been here.

And his gut gave a sickening lurch. Had she run? Because of him?

She'd been happy. He could have sworn he'd left her happy. The memory of the night before was all around him.

It had been dumb. He knew that. It had been spontaneous and stupid and…wonderful.

It had made him feel like he hadn't felt in… for ever?

He shouldn't have left her. He should have stayed this morning and talked.

And now she'd gone? This reeked of fear. Hell, did she think he was going to try and jump her? Push himself on her? Push past the boundaries they both knew were in place?

He stood in the empty bedroom and felt sick.

Finally he turned and headed back to the living room. There was a note on the mantel. He snatched it and read with hands that weren't quite steady. The thought of her heading away in fear was doing his head in.

She hadn't. It wasn't quite that bad.

Dear Noah.

Or should I make that Darling Noah after last night?

It was truly awesome, wasn't it? Just exactly what I needed and wanted and, oh, I loved it. But, wow, did we get carried away! We made love like out-of-control teenagers. I can't believe we were both that dumb.

But, to be honest, I don't regret it for a minute. Maybe it was what we both needed— good honest sex, no holds barred, a letting go for both of us before we move on.

But we do need to move on, Noah. We both do, and getting more enmeshed with each other will help neither of us. You have four months to go before whatever happens with Sophie, and you move on to wherever that decision takes you. I need to take up my role again, working in this community with commitment.

Noah, I need to get my head into that space again, and the bottom line, the truth I faced this morning, is that I can't get my head into that space if I continue sharing a house with you.

Something happened last night that took me way out of control. The thought of what we shared last night... Well, control doesn't come into it. One glass of wine—or even no glass of wine—and I run a very real chance of jumping you—and that's a crazy thought. I can't believe I'm admitting I'm scared, but I am, and therefore I'm taking steps to prevent it.

So I've rented a cottage. This is no big deal, Noah. No sacrifice. It's a wee cottage only two blocks from the hospital. Three minutes' walk. It's little, it's comfy and it has a spectacular view of the sea.

I thought about renting it when I first came here, but there was a bit of pressure to use the doctors' house and it did seem sensible. But I checked this morning and it's still available. It's fully furnished. The owners are happy for me to take it for four months, with the option of longer if I love it. As I suspect I might.

So me and my puppy and my new suitcase have gone down the road and that's us settled.

And you... Noah, you have a great place to stay for four months, too. We get to meet as colleagues—and, I hope, friends. But no more. We need to keep our hands and bodies under control. Sensible R Us.

Please don't think I'm making sacrifices, Noah. Believe it or not, I'm much happier today than I was yesterday. Sex with you blew away ghosts I hardly knew I had. So, thank you and let's move on.

But, Noah, I do need to talk to you about something very specific, and what I have to say can't be said over the phone. Would you consider fish and chips at my place? No wine!!! Directions below.

If you can't make it, don't worry, I'll catch up with you in the morning, but it needs to be soon.

Addie

He stood and stared at the note for a long time. It was a sensible note. A note designed to make him feel okay.

If she'd told him her intentions he would have offered to leave himself—he *would* have left himself—but she'd clearly had somewhere in mind where she could go.

He looked around the tidy, empty house and he felt…

Desolate?

Surely that was the wrong word. One night of sex did not a relationship make. Addie was being sensible and he had to match it.

She wanted to talk to him.

Fish and chips. Addie.

On the surface, it seemed a good plan. They had to become…friends? Nothing more.

'So she's made it easy for you.' He spoke out

loud and the room echoed. 'She's put us where we can become friends.'

If that's all you can have...the voice whispered at the back of his head, and he put it firmly aside.

Addie.

Why did she want to talk to him?

Friends.

Fish and chips.

He pulled out his phone. The hospital secretary had filled his list of colleague contacts and Addie was there.

She answered on the second ring.

'Noah?' She sounded uncertain. Scared even? But he could hear her collect herself, gather her containment. 'Hi.'

Deep breath. Keep it as she wanted it, he told her. *Friends.*

'How's the house?' he managed.

'Great. Fully furnished. We're all settled, and you should see the view from my back step.'

'Excellent.'

'But...' She sounded scared. 'I still... Noah, I do need to talk.'

'Half an hour? Your back step? But you're

right about no wine,' he told her. 'Not even a beer. You've made a sensible choice, Addie, and I concur. It's time we started acting like adults. Fish and chips on the back step and then back to our respective homes.'

'You bring the fish and chips. I'll supply the soda water.'

'A Saturday night to end all Saturday nights,' he said dryly, but he had to agree. They were both being…sensible. 'I'll put on my button-up shirt and my sensible boots and be right over.'

CHAPTER SEVEN

HER BACK STEP was gorgeous. Fabulous even. When she'd first thought of moving here she'd contacted the local realtor and he'd suggested this cottage. It was a simple cottage, with one bedroom, a kitchen/living room and basic bathroom, built to accommodate an elderly couple who came here occasionally to fish. But the couple had grown even more elderly. They could no longer travel from Sydney but were holding onto the house in the hope that their busy adult children might one day find time to use it. They paid cleaners to keep it neat, but they didn't much like the idea of tourists short-term renting.

Which meant the little cottage sat unoccupied, which was a shame. It had a gorgeous log fire. It had a lawn that ran down almost to the beach.

It had a view from the back step that took her breath away.

She sat there now, looking at the reflected rays of sunset over the ocean.

She waited.

Daisy had been tearing around, investigating every nook and cranny of her new home. She'd passed out now in her basket on the veranda. Happy.

And Addie was waiting for Noah.

For a friend, she reminded herself. Nothing more.

Except…

Don't go there.

More and more, she knew that she must.

And then he was there, opening the side gate, smiling a welcome, and she thought, *This* is the entire problem. This smile…

'You should have rung the doorbell,' she complained as Daisy lifted a weary head to investigate, decided it was only Noah and she could go back to sleep.

Only Noah.

'You did say your back step.' He paused and looked out at the sea, taking in the sweeping vista before him. 'Wow. I'm getting why you moved.'

'I hope you do.'

'I do.' He came and sat beside her. There was an ancient settee on the veranda and a table of sorts but the steps seemed somehow…better. She shifted a little, allowing him to set down his aromatic white package between them. Was there a more enticing smell in the world than hot fish and chips? She retrieved glasses and soda water from behind her, and a handful of paper napkins.

'Dinner's ready,' she said in contentment, and that was suddenly how she felt.

Like the night had settled. Like it was going to be okay.

Except…what she had to say.

Not yet.

They ate in silence, but not because there was tension. In fact, it was almost the opposite. What had happened between them should have created expectations, worry and, yes, sexual arousal, and maybe it had, but for some reason here in this place, for this moment, it had dissipated. All that was left was peace.

And food. Currawong fish and chipper had a reputation nationwide. Deservedly.

They ate tiny fillets of flathead, which was, in Addie's opinion, the world's most delicious fish, with a homemade tartare sauce that was mouthwatering. 'And it's sustainable,' Addie murmured as she popped the third piece into her mouth, and Noah grinned as he did the same.

'Excellent. Take nothing but photographs. Leave nothing but footprints.'

'And tread lightly on the planet,' she agreed as she eyed a gorgeous, buttery scallop. 'These are in season for such a short time but yum!'

The chips were magnificent as well, crisp, golden and so moreish she could have eaten twice as much, but there were fried onion rings and tiny potato cakes and a crisp garden salad so she had to somehow organise her priorities. Some of the chips had to be abandoned. With regret.

And then Noah produced tubs of chocolate ice cream. The ice cream had been slowly melting while they tackled the fish and chips. Now it'd reached the semi-solid state where it was creamy and melty. Even though Addie was full, the ice cream slithered into the edges.

Fantastic.

She ate and Noah ate, too, but she was aware he was watching her.

The sexual tension hadn't gone away. It was zinging in at the edges. Disguised as the taste of melting chocolate on her tongue?

She should focus on that rather than on Noah.

Like that was possible.

Finally she scraped the last of her ice cream from her tub and put it aside. Done.

And she needed to be done with the tension.

'I should make a pot of tea,' she said. 'Though I suspect I'll waddle as I walk inside and it's not a good look for a colleague.'

He chuckled and that was a good sound. A great sound. She loved his chuckle.

This should be okay, she thought. This was the start of acting…like friends. All she had to do was say goodnight and go inside.

But first there was the imperative.

Did she have to ask?

She knew she did.

Oh, but she didn't want to.

Her heart was screaming at her to do nothing, say nothing, but she'd been sensible all day. Her head was telling her to go on being sensible. Her heart had had its turn last night, and look at the mess that had landed her in. It was time for her head to say it like it was.

The sunset had faded. A crescent moon was rising over the horizon. She could just see the evening star.

No. It's Venus, she thought, or was it Jupiter? She could never remember. Either way it was a planet, not a star. So it's not an 'evening star' at all, she told herself. Get real.

And reality was?

Break the silence.

Say it.

'Noah, I didn't just ask you here for fish and chips.'

'You know, I guessed that,' he said, and she heard a hint of laughter. She loved that laughter. It did something…

Um, not. Focus on…not laughter.

'The reason I asked you here…' She sounded a bit desperate but that was how she was feeling. But she had to say it like it was.

'Noah, what was between us, what happened last night…we were well out of control and, to be honest, remembering the way I responded to you, it terrifies me. That's why I moved out. Neither of us are in the market for relationships. You need to be focussed on your access fight for Sophie. I've only just pulled myself together.'

'I understand. I felt bad until I saw this place but now…it makes sense.'

'But that's not all.' How to make herself say these next few words?

'Not?'

'No.' Deep breath. 'Noah, this morning… I went down to pharmacy and got the morning-after pill. I promised you I'd take it. That promise stands—if you want it. But now… I'm asking if you'll…reconsider.'

And she tugged the pill packet out of her jeans pocket and laid it on the step between them.

What followed was silence. A really long silence. It stretched out between them while the evening star got itself a few mates.

They were sitting on the middle step, with

the detritus of their makeshift picnic between them. And now a foil container.

What had she just landed him with?

A tiny possibility. The remotest of chances.

Why did it feel huge?

'Noah, this isn't fair,' she managed at last. She knew it wasn't. 'After all you've been through with Rebecca, with the way you've been manipulated, the last thing you need is me doing the same. I should just take it, move on. But I find… Noah, I can't make myself do it. Not without…asking.'

'You want to be pregnant?' Despite the lengthy silence his words were a blast of pure shock.

Say it like it was. 'Yes.' This much at least she knew for a fact. 'I do.'

'You're kidding.' His voice turned to incredulity. *'You planned this?'*

'Of…course I didn't,' she managed. 'Noah, we both know that. You must know it.'

For a moment she thought he'd get up, walk away, kick something. The look on his face was indescribable.

Fleetingly she remembered the moment she'd

slapped him. She'd been out of control. That's how Noah looked now.

But there was no slap. There was only more silence. She watched as he visibly sorted through what she'd said.

Finally he nodded. The incredulous look on his face faded. It seemed her version of last night's events had been accepted.

'I know that.'

Her world settled, a little. 'We just...'

'Came together out of mutual need.' The menace had gone, but the shock was still there. His voice turned calm again. Almost thoughtful. 'So...if a pregnancy comes of last night, you want to go through with it?'

She found she was shaking. She had to pull herself together. She had to explain.

'Noah, after the ectopic... After so many tries with IVF, so much failure, I thought I'd moved on. My pup, my suitcase and my new hairstyle, they were supposed to be the beginnings of my way forward. It was only this morning, staring at the pill, I thought, What am I doing? The possibility of pregnancy is so remote that it's almost laughable, but to kill that tiny chance...

I thought, What if I am pregnant? And it was like a shaft of light.'

He was staring at her as if he was staring at a future she'd just complicated a thousandfold.

'But I'd be the father,' he said blankly.

'You would.' She'd been thinking of this all day. Now she had to work out how to get her thoughts out there.

She glanced at him and then glanced away again. She had to say this without emotion, and looking at his face didn't help.

'Noah, if I was…then this *would* be your baby. That's why this has to be your decision, whether I take it or not. That's why I asked you to come tonight. I think…likely or not, the decision to proceed has to be yours as well.'

He was looking at her blankly, as if he could scarcely understand what she was saying. 'What…? Addie, I can't make you take it. It's your body.'

'It is, but if you ask me to take it then I will. And honestly… I'd take it with no regrets. Noah, I might go back to IVF. I might try again with sperm donation. What I do will be nothing to do with you. But this one slim chance…

it's your call. No matter what, I hope we'll still be colleagues. Still…friends? All I'll be doing by taking the pill is preventing something that probably won't happen anyway.'

'So…you're asking me, why?'

'I should have taken it this morning. It was only…suddenly it seemed big. And it did seem…as if it wasn't just my decision.'

'And if you don't take it?' His voice seemed to be coming from far away. 'If you are pregnant?'

'Then you'd have to decide how much you wanted to be involved.' She'd thought this through while she'd packed and moved, while she'd made up her new bed, while she'd sat on the back step and stared at nothing. 'If it does, if I am…you'd be within your rights…no, you'd be welcome to be a proper dad. To be as involved as you want. Noah, I understand Sophie's your priority and I respect that. We could work around it. Figure it out as we went along. But, Noah, I'm not Rebecca. I would never use a child to manipulate or control.'

'You have thought this through.'

'I've had all day,' she said ruefully. 'And my

head's been spinning. But I also need to say…
Noah, what's between you and me…our love-
making…that was a one-time thing. I have no
intention or wish to develop a relationship beyond co-parenting, and if you didn't want to
co-parent then that's okay, too. I had things organised in my head before I got pregnant last
time. I think I'll make a decent single mum.
I have huge community support, so I'd never
think less of you if you don't want contact. Neither will I think less of you if you sit with me
now while I swallow this pill. And I will take
it. If that's… what you want.'

But then…the shaking got worse.

Despite the warmth of the evening, the comfort of the food, she couldn't stop the tremors.
What was she asking of him? What sort of decision? She had every right to do this for herself, she thought, but she had no right to do it
to Noah.

But suddenly his hand was over hers, his fingers encircling, warm, firm, strong. His hand
held in a grip that was a message all by itself.

'You'd love to be pregnant.'

'Yes,' she said truthfully. 'But it's not my right—'

'If you had it…' His words cut her off '…I couldn't walk away. Addie, regardless of how our baby was conceived, I would care for you. I'd care for you both.'

'Like you were forced to care for Rebecca?' Where had that come from?

'No, I—'

'See, that's what I don't want.' Suddenly a new set of emotions were surfacing. She hauled her hand away from his as if it burned. 'Noah, you could care for our baby all you want—but not for me.' This situation was doing her head in. Was he offering…what he'd just walked away from?

Of course he was. This was Noah the honourable. Noah who'd tried to explain away Gavin's appalling behaviour. Noah who'd rung the day after the wedding fiasco to 'see if there's any way I can help…' Noah who'd stuck to his horrible wife. Noah who'd been betrayed in the most horrible way, and yet here he was with his hand up again.

I would care for you.

She should be impressed. She should think what a noble man.

Instead…

'I don't need to be cared for,' she managed, and she couldn't prevent a spurt of anger. 'Noah, thank you, but I don't want it.'

And then she caught herself. The last thing Noah deserved was anger—it was totally un-justified—but it'd been a huge day. She was overwrought and there was something about him that threatened her precious control.

He scared her?

The whole situation scared her. She had to haul herself together.

She had to explain her almost visceral response to his offer to care.

The truth? It seemed this was the night for it.

'Noah, you don't get it and you need to,' she managed. 'Caring's been my whole life. From the moment my dad died I was the carer. "Hug me, Addie," Mum would say. "Without you I couldn't go on." And… "Study hard, Addie. Your father was so smart and you're all I have left of him." And then Gavin… "Addie, marry Gavin… You'd make all our dreams come true.

You can't bring your father back, but to have his grandchildren… I could go to my grave happy…"'

Somehow she hauled herself back from the emotions threatening to overwhelm her. 'Noah, I suspect you know what I'm talking about. I can imagine the guilt Rebecca exposed you to, because I was exposed to it, too. And here you are, offering more of the same. You'll care for me and a possible baby because you're honourable. Noah, I don't want or need your care. You need to make a decision, but my need doesn't come into it.'

That brought more silence.

In the stillness Daisy woke. She'd been in her basket near the door. Now she wriggled across the veranda on her belly, as if she was unsure of her welcome. Addie was dimly aware of her but too caught in the moment to do anything about it. Unchecked, the little dog slithered over to the top step, wriggled her head down to the chip wrapper, seized a chip and bolted back to her basket.

Neither of them noticed.

The silence went on.

The little foil packet lay untouched.

'You don't think,' Noah said at last, and astonishingly there was suddenly a trace of a smile in his voice, 'you might be overreacting?'

Of course she was, but she wasn't backing down.

'All I'm saying is that I went into the IVF process with planning in place, with my future as a single mum sorted. So now…if anything were to happen, don't you dare think of me as an obligation. You have plans, too, Noah. If you don't get custody of Sophie, if it ends up that you can't even get access, then maybe it's time you had life as a carefree bachelor. You surely deserve it. So, Noah, if you want me to take the pill, I will. Here and now, while you watch me. Or tomorrow morning if you need time to think about it. You…we…have a forty-eight-hour window to decide.'

And that was enough. He was too close. She was feeling too emotional.

'Please…let's leave it,' she said, almost roughly. 'If you need to, think about it overnight. Know that whatever you decide there'll be no regrets. No blame. We'll both move on. But for now I need to go to bed.'

But then Daisy, emboldened by her initial slithery hunt, decided that discretion was for dummies. The chip had been delicious. She did another tummy-on-the-ground foray to the top step, but then looked down, saw Addie's hand poised to wrap the remaining chips—and made a flying bid to rescue the lot.

Puppy and chips and paper went flying, the pup somersaulting down the last four stairs. She lay stunned at the bottom, her legs in the air. A chip landed on her chin.

The chip went down the hatch, her tail gave an enormous wiggle like she'd just achieved something spectacular and she rolled over and proceeded to pounce on the remains.

It was so comical they both had to laugh, and it was what they both needed. Over-the-top emotion receded as they cleared the mess. When it was done, Noah's face was calm again. Under control.

'We're talking of a situation that in all prob-ability won't happen,' he said. 'Let's keep it calm.'

'Let's.' Maybe she should say more but it was all she could think of.

'I need to head back to the hospital.'

'I... Yes. Thank you for the fish and chips.'

'Thank you for the hospitality.'

They stood, motionless. She'd picked Daisy up. She had her in her arms and she was holding her almost like a shield.

Why?

Because she wanted...what? She was afraid of what?

She was afraid of what she was feeling.

The pregnancy issue aside, what she was feeling right now...

She wanted more of what she'd had last night.

Which was why she'd moved out of the doctors' house.

'Goodnight, Noah,' she managed. 'And don't...please don't build this into a big deal. It's nothing. Just let me know.'

'It's not nothing.'

'I won't be pregnant.'

'Even if you aren't pregnant, it's still *not nothing*.' He put a hand out and cupped her face, a gesture of...what? She didn't know. All she knew was that his touch made her whole body quiver. She had to step back and she did.

'It's not nothing and you know it,' he said gently. 'And you know what? There's also a part of me that'd accept pregnancy with joy. But let's worry about tomorrow when tomorrow comes.' He smiled into her eyes, that mesmeric smile that did something to her heart that she'd never felt before. 'Meanwhile, I don't know about you but I had very little sleep last night. Let's do better tonight.'

And he chucked Daisy under one of her soft ears. He smiled again at Addie, a smile directed straight at her.

And then he took the foil packet and tucked it into his top pocket. 'I'll take this with me,' he said. 'Pharmacy can dispose of a drug we have no need of.'

He walked home along the cliff path, his hands deep in his pockets, his thoughts back in the little house he'd just left. He'd left his car at the hospital because it was a five-minute walk via the fish shop and he'd needed to walk. He needed a walk even more now. He took the long route around the headland, a thirty-minute hike, and even that wasn't long enough to get his head together.

What had just happened?

It hadn't just happened, though, he thought. It had happened last night, when he'd taken Addie into his bed, into her bed. And she'd taken him. The sex had been mind-blowing, the release of years of frustration, anger, need. The release of years of...caring?

But now the caring was right back with him. His concern for her...

She probably wasn't pregnant but if she was, she'd made her decision. And he'd made his.

She...they...wanted a baby.

He paused and stared out over the blackness of the ocean. The moon created a sliver of silver over the waves but the water still looked dark, empty, threatening.

His baby.

Addie.

'You're talking of something that won't happen,' he told himself, but that sounded wrong, too.

And yet...it was probably right. He'd done a

statistics unit once to help with research he was undertaking. He understood odds.

The odds said he was out here talking to himself about something that would never happen.

But if it did…

'Then you'll cope with it,' he said, still aloud. But then…she'd already made a declaration that she wouldn't need him.

Would he be sidelined again in a child's life?

She'd sworn that he wouldn't, and somehow he believed her.

So…did he want her to be pregnant? Wasn't his life complicated enough?

'Yes, it is. So why take the pill home with you?'

Because she wants a baby, he argued within himself.

'Do you? Are you trying to replace Sophie?'

The thought made his gut clench and he knew it wasn't true. Sophie was irreplaceable and always would be.

'You're being dumb,' he said, still out loud. 'Let's not dramatise something that won't happen. This is not a worry.'

He moved on, but as he did so he thought it wasn't exactly worry.

It was more like...hope?

CHAPTER EIGHT

Ten days later...

IT'S SAID THE *gods laugh at those who play the odds.*

The odds said she couldn't be pregnant.

Someone up there was definitely laughing.

She walked out to the back step, increasingly her favourite place in the world, and sat down.

Hard.

Daisy bolted across the lawn to join her. Addie laid the plastic tester aside—carefully, as if it might break. She took her little dog into her arms and hugged.

And started to shake.

She'd been down this road before and it had ended in heartbreak. But hope was lying beside her in the form of two blue lines on a piece of plastic.

She set Daisy down. The little dog headed

off into the garden to see if she could dig down to a cricket chirping just under the lawn surface. She should stop her. Who needed holes in lawns? But she wasn't thinking of the lawn now. She picked up the sliver of plastic again and the lines were still there. She was pregnant and all she could feel was terror.

Terror for herself?

'Please…' It was a desperate whisper from somewhere deep within her. It was a plea and a prayer and an admission that she was way out of control. She'd never meant this. She could have stopped it. She should have…

No. She dropped the plastic and her hands went to her belly, instinctively, in the way of mothers the world over.

Her baby.

Please…

She'd have to tell Noah. This decision had been his as well as hers.

This was his baby.

But…but…

There was no reason to tell him. Not yet. She was literally days into her pregnancy. The problem with increasingly sophisticated pregnancy tests was that they confirmed pregnancy ridiculously early. She knew better than anyone the odds of miscarriage. Most miscarriages occurred almost before the mother suspected she was pregnant. If there was a problem, a woman's body was wired to rid itself of a non-viable pregnancy, clearing the way to start again.

But please... Not this time. Let there be no problem.

She did have to tell Noah.

Tell him what? She was talking to herself almost hysterically. Should she tell him that she was two minutes pregnant?

She should wait and see.

But she knew she couldn't. It was his right to know.

And that was doing her head in. She wanted this baby so much, and somehow she'd dragged him right in. Noah, with his overblown sense of obligation, his friendship. His...his...

She couldn't go there. There was so much about Noah she didn't understand, so much that almost frightened her. She wasn't in control when he was around.

So many emotions...

Daisy got bored and started pouncing on her knees from the steps above. Over and over. Every time she pounced, Addie picked her up and set her down, which suited Daisy fine.

Babies liked repetition.

Baby…

Her mind seemed like it was caught in an out-of-control spin that left her feeling almost nauseous. She should be joyously happy, but there were so many unknowns. So much fear.

And Noah.

Noah's baby.

Where to go from here?

Pretend things were normal? Wait and see? Decisions seemed impossible and when her phone rang she was almost grateful.

What she needed until she had her head under control was work. A lovely birth, with no major complications but tricky enough to take her mind off what she could barely hope to think about. She had three mums due to give birth about now. Hopefully one was about to oblige.

'Addie?'

But it was Noah and simply by the way he said her name she knew this wasn't a friendly chat.

Neither was it a call about a normal delivery. There was urgency behind the two syllables.

Medicine. Her world. She was already shoving her feet back into her shoes, heading indoors with the phone in her hand. 'Give.'

'Car accident,' he told her. 'Car clipped a lorry and rolled. They're bringing them in now. Briana and Tom Danvers. Briana's suffered multiple injuries and Morvena says she's one of yours. The paramedics say she's in final trimester.'

Addie knew her. She'd seen her two days ago for her prenatal check. Bouncy and confident, Briana had been the picture of health, and the pregnancy was totally normal. 'She's thirty-four weeks,' she said, grabbing her car keys.

'They're thinking foetal distress. They couldn't get a heartbeat at first but it's there now. It could be inexperience that had them not hearing, or stress, but we need you here.'

'Of course. Where's the ambulance? Can I meet it on the way?' She didn't say—she didn't have to say—that the most common injury to a baby in a car crash was placental abruption.

If the placenta completely separated from the uterus then death of the baby was inevitable, but if there was a heartbeat now, that hadn't happened. A likely scenario was partial abruption, which meant a partial tear. If the oxygen supply was blocked for any length of time, or even intermittently...

She had to reach her fast.

'They'll be here in five minutes.'

Five minutes meant there was no advantage to meeting the ambulance for roadside intervention. 'I'm on my way. Other injuries?'

'Tom has lacerations, concussion, query broken collar bone. Briana has a broken wrist and chest injuries. Breathing issues. Query broken ribs. The pregnancy means they haven't been able to give her anything.'

'They can give her morphine if they need to. There's crossover but it's better than having her in agony. Airway stabilisation's a priority but they know that. I'm there in three minutes. Or less.'

And she was out the front door, leaving a bewildered Daisy looking sadly after her. Addie had been about to take her over to spend the afternoon with the oldies but there was no time to organise it now. 'I'll be with you before the ambulance.'

Morvena might be autocratic, dogmatic, even ruthless, but in a crisis there was no one doctors depended on more than a good nurse manager. She'd obviously mustered the troops. Addie reached the hospital before the ambulance arrived, and two other cars were screeching into the car park. Cliff, the anaesthetist, and Rob Holloway, the youngest of the town's family physicians.

Four doctors. Cliff and Rob for Tom, Noah and her for Briana? Swap Cliff when needed? If Tom's brain injury was severe it'd have to be Noah and Cliff with Tom, and Rob with her. She was already playing out an emergency Caesar, planning resources.

She headed straight for the trauma room. Noah was before her. Cliff and Rob had veered off to Emergency admissions. There was no greeting. There was no time for anything but what lay ahead.

'Briana's ours,' Noah snapped. 'The paramedics say she's short of breath and they can feel broken ribs. There's also blocked circulation to the arm, plus the foetal problems. I'm scrubbing for an immediate thoracostomy if that's necessary. Our priorities are assessment, breathing, baby, wrist.'

Her skill was babies. Delivering babies. Fast. Noah was the generalist and this was his call.

She nodded her agreement. Noah was prioritising on the paramedic's information but it was a reasonable call. They could change their minds after initial assessment but it settled them all to have an initial plan, to know what they were facing.

Morvena was standing in the background, holding her phone, waiting for orders. Addie might have had puppy issues with this woman, but she had no issues now.

'I need everything for a stressed premmie,' she told her. 'Incubator, the works. See if you can get one of the other GPs in, in case we need help with the baby. Warm everything. And ring the flying neonatal squad from Sydney. We can always call them off if we don't need them.'

'Already done,' Morvena said.

'Tell them to add another doctor to the flying squad,' Noah told her. 'A trauma specialist as well as a paediatrician. If we need to evacuate a distressed premmie and a mum with breathing problems, plus Tom with possible head injuries, we'll need full medical support.'

'If a thoracostomy tube's needed, can we evacuate by air?' Addie asked tentatively. This was not her specialty so she needed to ask. Did they need to organise a road ambulance as back-up? Noah gave her a swift nod of acknowledgement. Doctors questioning each other was never a problem—it made for far fewer mistakes.

'It's okay,' he told her. 'As long as the tube's in situ and they fly at low altitude there's no problem. Morvena...'

'I'm onto it,' Morvena said. 'I'll ring in more nurses.'

She wheeled away. Addie headed for the sinks.

Two minutes later the scream of the ambulance siren filled the silence of the valley and it was on.

* * *

The paramedics' assessment had been—was—totally accurate. They wheeled Briana in first and one look showed she was in deadly trouble. She was breathing fast. Her chest was heaving with effort, and her eyes were wide with panic. Noah was already in scrubs, gloved. While Noah watched, Addie pushed away the thermal blanket they'd used to keep her warm, then carefully removed the collar the paramedics had used in case of neck fracture. They both looked at her trachea and the shift was obvious. It was displaced, moved to the side.

Tension pneumothorax.

The paramedics had already slit her T-shirt. A light feel of her chest suggested the likelihood of rib fracture. Piercing of the lung. Air was obviously escaping, building up in the chest and causing the lungs to collapse.

There was also the complication of her left wrist. Briana's hand was pallid, cold and pulseless.

Circulation?

Breathing first.

Addie was examining her ribs, gently feeling,

focussing on the break. Briana was wild-eyed, terrified, frantic. To not be able to breathe…

Addie took her good hand and held it, taking a sliver of a moment to give human contact, to make Briana feel like she was being held. That the fight was no longer hers.

'You're okay now, Briana. Safe. Try and relax while we ease your breathing.'

'Briana, the reason you're having trouble breathing is that you have air in your chest.' Noah's voice followed hers, deep, calm, steady. They were both in Briana's line of vision, but her gaze locked on Noah. 'It looks like you've broken a rib and it's letting air in, squashing your lung. It feels terrifying but it's easy to fix. The first thing we'll do—what I'll do now— is put a tube into your chest to let the air out.'

'But Tom…' It was a frantic gasp.

'Tom's okay.' Once again his calm, deep voice got through. This wasn't a voice that could be argued with. 'He's copped a few cuts and bruises and a broken collar bone but we think he'll be fine. Dr Holloway and Dr Brooks are taking care of him but they're not bringing him in here. He's bleeding a bit and Morvena doesn't like blood on her nice clean trauma room, do you, Morvena?'

There was a snort from that lady behind them and Addie almost smiled. But...

'My baby...' Briana gasped.

'Yep, we'll check on her, too,' Noah said calmly. 'Her? Him? Do we know?'

'H-her.'

'Nice,' Noah said, and smiled. 'The ambulance officers have checked on your baby's heartbeat, and it's nice and loud.' There was no point in telling her there could be a problem. 'So our first priority is to get your breathing sorted. You have a broken wrist, too, Briana, and you need to let us sort it, but that comes second. I'm about to pop a needle in to get rid of the extra air in your lung. Then X-ray. Then we'll look at your wrist. It must be hurting like hell. We can fix that. Okay with you, Briana?'

He was gazing straight down at Briana, eyes locked on hers, and Addie saw the moment the panic eased.

Trust...

Briana trusted this man, and why wouldn't she? There was no hesitation, only certainty that this was the way to go.

He'd downplayed nothing. He'd told the exact truth. Too much air in your lung, let's get rid of it. Your baby's alive, we'll check on her. Your wrist is broken, we'll fix it.

'We need to do a bit of undressing,' Noah told Briana, and he summoned one of his gorgeous smiles. 'It's undignified, I know, but needs must. Addie needs to listen to that baby of yours and I need complete access to your chest. Sorry, but that very attractive T-shirt is about to become ribbons. Jeans, too.'

'They're my...they're my gardening clothes,' Briana wheezed. 'We were going home...from helping my mother...spread chook poo on her roses.'

'Well, I'm very sorry, but your chook-poo-spreading T-shirt and jeans are no more,' Noah said gently. He couldn't touch her as he was already gloved, but Addie was doing the touching for him. 'But let's mourn them later. First let's get you safe.'

While Noah worked, Addie was fully occupied with her role, setting up a foetal monitor, trying to get a handle on the condition of the baby.

She wasn't liking what she was finding.

The paramedics had mentioned when they'd first tried for a heartbeat that they hadn't been able to find one. Given the roadside conditions, given the mother's distress, given their own stress, they could well have missed it. The second time they'd tried they'd found it but it was erratic. Addie took blood for cross-matching straight away as a precaution and then set up a foetal heart monitor. She studied the cardiotocography and found no reassurance.

There were dips in the baby's heart rate.

Briana had been hit, hard, and the placenta would have been slammed within the abdomen.

There was also vaginal bleeding. Not much, but enough for deep concern.

If this was partial abruption, it could turn to full at any moment. Or damage alone would be enough to cause foetal death. She needed to see this baby. She needed to be hands on.

This was a thirty-four-week pregnancy. Totally viable. The risks on leaving her in situ were enormous.

She wanted this baby born now.

Her eyes met Noah's and held for a fraction

of a moment. It didn't take longer. He read the message.

He was working swiftly himself, with skill and precision, to establish a secure airway.

A local anaesthetic came first, then prophylactic antibiotics to prevent complications like pneumonia later. Finally the chest tube was inserted carefully, and at last Addie heard the blessed hiss of released air, the instant relief of a compressed lung.

Briana's short, frantic gasps eased.

Panic receded.

Then Cliff was in the room, swinging in with the casual air of a doctor who was there for a social visit. He was good, too, Addie thought, and thanked her lucky stars for such colleagues. His presence meant they had three doctors. It must also mean that Tom was safe. Her stress level dropped a notch.

'Greetings, all,' the anaesthetist said, smiling down at Briana. 'Mrs Danvers, you and your husband have interrupted my attendance at my son's under-twelve footie match. We're winning forty-seven to three and my Lucas has kicked seven goals. I need to get back for the riotous celebration of sausage rolls and soda. Meanwhile, I've been in to see your Tom. He's bruised and bumped and he has a sore shoulder but he's okay. I've given him a nice little something so he can be stitched up without pain and Dr Holloway has taken over. Now it's your turn. What do you need me here for, guys?'

'X-ray next.' Noah was adjusting the thoracostomy tube, responding to Cliff but still talking to Briana. Including her in the conversation. Holding her to him in a way that surely must settle her in the midst of pain and fear. 'Briana, your wrist is broken and needs to be reset. Dr Blair—Addie—also needs to run checks on your baby. What we plan to do is run you through X-ray, maybe do an ultrasound of your baby, and then make a decision.'

He hesitated but only for a fraction of a moment, a fraction that Briana wouldn't have picked up on but Addie heard it. It was a pause that meant he'd picked up on Addie's concern. And it was best to be honest.

'Briana, we'll need to put you under in order to treat your wrist,' he told her. 'You have a blocked blood supply to your fingers and if we leave that for long you might end up with long-term stiffness.' Paralysis, he meant, but that was a scary word to use. 'But more.' He nodded to Addie, an acknowledgement that she should take over the conversation if he got it wrong.

'Briana, we're also going to do a very careful assessment of your baby. She's been given a fair shaking. She's thirty-four weeks. If she's born now then she's hardly even classified as premature. She's a fully formed baby, ready to be born. Ideally she'd probably choose to stay where she is for a few more weeks, but she's had a bump and we'd like to see her, to make sure she's okay. Dr Blair thinks the safest thing is to perform a Caesar. Would that be okay with you?'

'You'll take my baby...' Briana quavered, and Addie stooped so her face was close to Briana's. She touched her cheek, wiping away a frightened tear.

'No, Briana, we won't take your baby,' she told her. 'We'll give you your baby. I am a little worried,' she conceded. 'You have a bruise on your abdomen, which means you've been hit. I can hear your baby's heartbeat so she's okay but I don't know if you have internal bleeding. For now, though, you and Tom and your baby are safe and we plan to keep it that way, even if it means we bring your little girl into the world a bit early. You need to trust us. Will you do that, Briana?'

'I...' Briana looked wildly around, at Addie, at the stern-faced Morvena in the background, at the now-serious Cliff, and then lastly at Noah. She looked at him for a long time.

What was it with this man? Briana instinctively looked at him with trust.

Whatever it was, she was taking it, Addie thought, because she saw the moment Briana relaxed. She saw the moment Briana decided she could abandon her flight-and-fight reflex and just...trust.

'Okay,' Briana whispered. 'Just do it.'

And after that there was no time for introspection, no time for thoughts of anything other than doing.

The X-rays showed a comminuted fracture of the wrist. There was an intermittent pulse. If there hadn't been, in probability she'd be looking at the loss of her hand, but the paramedics had done their job well. They'd stabilised it, splinting it as well as they could, which had allowed a tiny amount of blood to get through.

Not enough to stay viable for long, though, and the X-rays showed it wasn't enough to depend on. The fracture meant she'd need specialist orthopaedic surgery to make sure the hand was fully functional but they needed to reduce the fracture now to make sure her hand was viable until they could get her to Sydney.

Meanwhile, the information Addie was accumulating was growing increasingly worrying. The vaginal bleeding was sluggish but constant, and the baby's heartbeat...

'Anaesthetic now,' she said, as the world's fastest X-ray and ultrasound were completed. She stooped and kissed Briana lightly on the cheek. It was totally unprofessional but she'd been this woman's doctor for over two years. She'd seen the joy of Briana and Tom when their pregnancy had been confirmed. How hard was it to stay aloof in such circumstances?

She couldn't.

So she kissed her and signalled to Cliff to take over at the top end, but before he took her place she smiled down into Briana's eyes.

'Time to let us take over, Briana,' she told her. 'Time to relax and trust us. When you wake up you'll have your baby.'

'You promise?'

There was a risk… This baby had been shaken… She couldn't see the extent of the injury.

But who was she to say that now? If there was major trauma, if the unthinkable happened, a promise made and broken would be something Addie was prepared to carry.

'I promise,' she said, and as she said it she was suddenly aware of a brush against her arm, the slightest of pressures.

Noah.

It was a hug that was hardly a hug.

That was hardly professional either, doctor hugging doctor, but there it was and she'd take it.

'We all promise,' Noah said gravely. 'Briana, can Cliff put you under now? Can we bring your baby into the world?' And panic took an even greater step back. Briana searched their faces, one after the other, and finally she sighed.

'Tom...'

'He's still making a mess of my emergency department,' Morvena told her. 'But the minute he's tidy we'll bring him in to meet his daughter. I promise that, too.'

And they all smiled. The grumpy Morvena was no one to argue with and Briana wasn't trying.

'So can I send you byebyes?' Cliff asked, and there was only one answer.

'Yes, please,' Briana whispered. 'I want... my baby.'

It was a crowded theatre.

While Addie worked to deliver the baby, Noah stabilised the thoracostomy tube. He was deferring to Addie, and that was a skill all on its own.

Egos often seemed something that came with the job description of surgeon. They played with lives under their hands every day, and without confidence they couldn't go on. But Noah had the mix right.

They had the screen up, separating work spaces, working as if Briana were awake and wouldn't want to watch the cutting process. In fact, it meant easier delineation, with less likelihood of cross-contamination between surgery sites. But Noah wasn't going ahead to align the wrist until the baby was delivered and the wound was closed. That'd be too big a risk. He did what he could to maintain circulation. Not for a minute did he let Addie think he was waiting. He knew she accepted the urgency.

They all did. Cliff was monitoring breathing, no easy task for a patient as compromised as Briana. Rob, the family doctor who'd attended Tom, had appeared as surgery had started. 'Tom's okay,' he told them. 'Worried but good. He's under obs and I'll head back if needed, but I thought you might want someone for the baby.'

Morvena was there. And Heidi.

They had a warmed incubator. They had paediatric resuscitation equipment.

Go.

Addie swabbed, then cut with the skill and

precision of years of training. She scooped in and lifted.

There was an audible intake of breath. Held. Until the first weak cry…

Which grew stronger. Indignation a plus!

One tiny, fragile but already-turning-pink baby girl had entered the world.

As Addie turned to hand her over to Rob— her priority had to be Briana as there was still danger of haemorrhage—she caught Noah's glance. Just for a moment. It was a fleeting glimpse, a shadow of expression.

Care?

More than care. Involvement. Total empathy.

Despite the intricacy of this operation, despite the concentration he had to apply, he had the whole room under surveillance. Did he know what each of them was thinking?

What made her believe he knew what she was thinking? She hardly knew herself. All she knew was that as she handed over the tiny bundle of new life into Rob's skilled hands, as she hesitated for just one fraction of a second, as she felt the tug of letting go…

She knew Noah was with her.

'Hey, she looks great.' Rob had her on the

pre-warmed pad, using suction to clear the tiny airway, performing a fast examination, looking for impact damage. 'She looks perfect.'

And for that tiny moment Addie's control slipped.

Perfect.

'Chopper's on its way with the neonatal squad,' Noah told Rob, but he was looking at Addie.

She got it.

He knew.

But the fraction of hesitation was past. She'd turned back to the operating table. Morvena was handing her the instruments she needed.

There was bleeding. Addie could see the damage to the uterus where the placenta had started separating.

They'd been so lucky. A new little life…

She was back at work, suturing, doing her darnedest to ensure that if Briana wanted future babies it'd be possible.

Doing her darnedest to make babies possible.

All the while she had a baby growing within her.

Noah's.

* * *

The helicopter took off an hour later. Aboard was a dazed but conscious Tom, an even more dazed but conscious Briana, and one tiny newborn called Alicia Adeline.

'Don't make any decisions until the drugs wear off,' Addie had told them when they'd told her the name, but Briana had smiled weakly and taken her hand.

'You were the last person I saw when I went to sleep and when I woke up, my baby was here,' she whispered. 'I'd like to use Noah, too, but that'll have to wait until next time.'

'And there will be a next time.' Noah stood next to Addie on the hospital veranda and watched as the chopper lifted. 'You've not only saved the baby,' he told Addie, 'I saw the way you stitched that uterus and I'd defy a second kid to rip that neat little bit of handiwork, no matter how hard he or she stretches. 'That's some skill you have, Dr Blair.'

'Speak for yourself, Dr McPherson.' She'd seen what he'd done with Briana's wrist. She'd seen the skill and surety of the thoracostomy tube. Most of all she'd seen the way he'd settled Briana's panic, and Tom's as well when he'd seen his wife and reacted with terror at the sight of the attached medical paraphernalia.

But now they were on their way to Sydney in the best of hands. Yes, tiny Alicia was prem and Briana would need further surgery, but all indications were that this was a happy ending.

For a moment Addie let herself relax. She closed her eyes and the emotions of the day took a step back.

She was standing on the veranda, with the feel of the afternoon sun on her face, the sound of the wash of the sea in her ears, the gentle talk of the oldies in the background…

The faintest of touches of Noah's body against hers.

And then his arm came around her and held.

'You're pregnant,' he said, and it wasn't a question.

CHAPTER NINE

SHE DIDN'T OPEN her eyes.

This was just an extension of what she was feeling, she thought. God was in his heaven, and all was right with her world.

She was pregnant.

'I am,' she whispered. 'About two minutes pregnant. Far too soon to...'

Far too soon to be sure of anything. Too soon to know if it was a viable pregnancy. Too soon to know if it was ectopic.

Too soon to tell if it was anything other than hope.

He'd know all those things.

He didn't say anything. For a long moment they simply stood. His hand wasn't possessive. It was simply a touch in the small of her back. Contact. Warmth.

Strength?

She needed to pull away, to let him know

she didn't need it. She didn't need him. So she would, in a moment, but just for now she let herself absorb his touch as part of the peace of this moment.

They'd just saved a little life.

There was a possibility of a little life between them.

There were, however, practicalities. Cliff and Rob were cleaning up inside. There were case notes to be written up—they'd sent brief notes with the chopper but a fax with details needed to be sent to Sydney Central, hopefully to arrive before the chopper did. Then the normal Saturday afternoon bumps and bruises from Currawong would be waiting.

The world was waiting.

She made a move to step away but suddenly Noah's hold firmed.

'You're not in this alone, Addie. This is a shared journey.'

She blinked. What had she expected him to say?

Was he laying claim to her baby? Maybe he was, but the way he'd said it…

'I can manage,' she was able to get out. 'I…

Even if it does…turn out to be viable…' she took a deep breath '…you know there's every chance I'll miscarry. Or it'll be another ectopic.'

'And there's every chance it won't.'

'I won't let myself go down that road yet. Maybe…in a couple of weeks…'

'Then we can find out whether it's in the right place.' He smiled down at her. 'A scan will be exciting—though it'll be too soon to tell if we're having a boy or a girl.'

If we're having…

We.

'It'll be too soon to tell anything other than whether the pregnancy's in utero or in the fallopian tubes,' she managed. 'At five weeks the pregnancy's just…a thing.'

A thing. Who was she kidding?

Her baby.

He'd said we.

'You don't need… Noah, if you want…this can be nothing to do with you. I never meant—'

'And neither did I,' he said. 'Neither of us planned this pregnancy, but it's happened and it's ours.'

'You didn't want this.'

'Did I say I didn't want this?' His gaze met hers, strong and sure. But there was a trace of something else. Implacability? 'Addie, you know darned well neither of us planned this—neither of us gave a thought to consequences. But it's happened, and you're feeling hope. And you know what? So am I.'

'But I don't want—'

'Me? Sorry, Addie, but you're stuck with me. You gave me assurances the night you didn't take the pill and I'm holding you to them. I'm darned if I'll be a sperm donor and back right out of your life. Out of our child's life.'

'But you're going back to Sydney. You have Sophie to care for. And if you lose access… You said England.'

'That might have to change.' He shrugged. 'Maybe it'd never happen anyway. Even if I don't have access…to walk away from Sophie… and now you…'

'Noah, you can't factor me into that equation. For one thing it's way too soon. It's crazy. And I don't need you. *I won't need you.*'

'So what do you mean by that?' he asked, and she was so out of control she told him.

'Noah, I can't,' she said. 'I told you… All my life my mum needed me. She needed me for everything. Her need controlled my life. I nearly married Gavin because of it. I was a doormat, a nothing. Need's no basis for anything. *I won't need you.*'

He stood and watched her, his face thoughtful. Kind? He was kind, she thought wildly. She could so easily…need.

No.

'That's why you went the sperm donor route?' he asked at last. 'Is that why you've steered clear of any relationship? Because you're scared of needing?'

'And being needed.' She fought for control, for sense, and managed a shamefaced smile. 'I'm sorry, Noah, I'm not making sense to you, but I'm making sense to me.'

'This baby will need you.'

'I can teach independence. I will.'

'Is that a priority? Independence?'

'It has to be. Noah…'

He saw her panic. She saw the moment he realised she was struggling for control.

She saw the moment he decided to back off.

'Let's leave it,' he said, gently now. 'It is too soon. We need to wait. We wait until the five-week mark until we find out for certain whether he or she is in utero or not. We wait until three months until we can do a decent scan and find out if our baby has all the right bits and pieces. And then we wait for forty or so weeks until we can welcome our child.'

Our child.

'Anything can happen,' she said miserably. 'You can't plan—'

'I won't plan,' he told her. 'I can only hope, as you're hoping. But whatever happens...' He sighed then and smiled but it was a tentative smile, a smile that said he was in unknown territory as much as she was. He put his hand up and traced her cheek with his forefinger, a feather touch that was maybe meant for reassurance but was maybe...much more?

'But whatever happens,' he repeated, 'you're not alone. Don't look so panicked, love,' he told her. 'I'm not about to take control, holding you down while you act as an incubator for my child. Major decisions are yours to make. I'm with you, though. You'll need—'

'I won't *need*.' Anger surged again—or was it fear? Emotions were threatening to overwhelm her. 'Don't group me with Rebecca, Noah. Don't you dare change your life because someone else needs you. I don't. I won't.'

'Our baby might.'

'Then that's…that's a contract between you and this baby. It's for you to work out in the future. Noah, I need to get back on an even keel. I have case notes to write and so do you. We need to get back to work.'

'But not ignore what's going on.'

'As best we can, yes,' she managed. 'Because I can't allow myself to hope.'

'Well, there's a lost cause,' he told her, and that smile flashed out again, the smile that was so dangerous it did her head in. 'Because both of us are hoping with everything in our hearts.' He hesitated. 'Addie…you wouldn't consider moving back into the doctors' house?'

'Why would I do that?'

'If it is an ectopic—'

'Then it's way too early for it to cause problems. Noah, back off. I'm darned if I'll have you staring at my tummy for the next forty weeks, waiting for something to explode.'

'I wouldn't do that. But I do care.'

'Then stop caring,' she said brusquely. 'Or maybe…care a little bit but not that much, and only care about the baby. Care from a distance and not for me. For now we both need to put our heads down and move forward.'

'But not together?'

'There's no *together*.'

And that brought a matching flash of anger. Or frustration? Maybe a mix of both. 'Addie, we now have a relationship, like it or not. That's my baby you're carrying.' But then he paused, maybe having heard how he'd sounded. Deciding to regroup? 'No. It's *ours*,' he said, more gently but just as firmly. 'Yours and mine, and I will be involved. There has to be some sort of relationship for that to happen.'

'Fine,' she managed, but she knew she sounded scared. 'I meant…just not a man and a woman relationship. Not a relationship based on need. That's over. I'm never going down that road again, and neither should you.'

* * *

The late afternoon and evening were busy and Noah was grateful. Thomas Emmanuel, aged seven, had come off his roller blades and fractured his arm. The greenstick fracture should have been easy to treat but Thomas's mother was hysterical with anxiety and his father was threatening to sue everyone, right down to the council who'd planted the trees in the park because it must have been the gum nuts on the path that had caused Thomas to fall. Their reactions had been transmitted to Thomas. By the time Noah saw him, the little boy was vomiting in fear and pain, and Noah could scarcely get near.

It took patience, time and finally authority to settle things. 'If you can't be calm for your son, if you can't let me work without interference, then Thomas will need to be evacuated to Sydney to be treated by a paediatric team. Is that what you wish?'

It wasn't. They backed off. He then had to spend time calming the little boy, getting him interested in what was going on, talking of how they could decorate his cast, until he could finally set his arm without resorting to general anaesthetic.

Finally it was done. Thomas left between his parents, carrying his braced arm like a trophy. It had its first decoration—a motor bike sticker Noah just happened to have on hand for such an occasion, and the boy was asking where he could get more. The rest of the day's odds and sods were sorted and Noah was free to go home.

To the doctors' house.

Which was empty.

He'd shared this house with Addie for less than a week. He'd been alone in it for almost two months before that.

Why did it feel so lonely tonight?

He ate the casserole Mrs Rowbotham had left him, then snagged a beer and went and sat on the front veranda. There were still lights on in some of the wards. There were people moving behind the drapes.

People…

He abandoned his beer and walked out of the hospital grounds, down to the beach beyond.

He was done with people. Except for Sophie.

Addie had it right when she said the last thing he wanted was someone else to need him.

He didn't.

But?

He was damned if he was going to leave her.

Why? Because he wanted this baby?

Yeah, okay, that was probably it. Something seemed to have died inside him the day Rebecca had told him he no longer had access to Sophie. Addie's news had been like a bolt from the blue, and now it felt like the most extraordinary gift.

And it wasn't all about the baby. In fact, it wasn't even mostly about the baby. The way Addie made him feel...

But he had to tread with care, he told himself. A woman he scarcely knew, a woman he'd... okay, say it like it was...a woman he'd shared a one-night stand with, was pregnant. She'd made her own decisions. He didn't owe her anything.

Except he did. She'd been vulnerable. She'd been...

Addie.

He could see the lights from her cottage from

where he stood on the beach. Was she still awake?

Surely it had nothing to do with him.

But it had to have something to do with him. He stood on the beach and let the shock of the day drift and settle.

There'd been too much emotion, he told himself. Neither of them needed it. What he needed was to be sensible.

If this pregnancy progressed to a birth then, regardless of what happened with Sophie, he couldn't go to London. He knew that.

But then he thought, even if this pregnancy didn't work out, how could he leave Addie? How could he walk away from her pain?

That was a bit of a blindsider.

Emotion… Back off, he told himself. Talk sense.

The light flicked off in the little cottage up on the cliff. She'd gone to bed.

She'd be frightened.

Of course she would. Even without the unknowns of her pregnancy, he'd threatened her. He'd seen it in her body language. She didn't need him. Or…she didn't want to need him.

But friends... If he could figure that one out...

Where to start?

His mind was in overdrive.

He paced a while longer. This was important. He needed to get things right.

CHAPTER TEN

ON SUNDAY ADDIE woke to Daisy going nuts at the door, almost turning inside out with excitement. She heard footsteps on the veranda. A knock.

She pushed back the curtains, just a little, and saw Noah standing at her front door. Casually dressed in jeans and T-shirt, he was grinning at the noise on the other side of the door.

Noah. Here.

She glanced at her watch and gasped. Ten! She'd slept and slept.

A first sign of pregnancy was often weariness.

Her hand flew instinctively to her belly. She was pregnant. She was still pregnant!

And her baby's father was standing at her front door.

It was no use pretending she wasn't home when Daisy was making mad dashes to her bedroom, to the door, to the bedroom, to the door, yipping in excitement. She shoved her feet into flip-flops, grabbed her glasses, then glanced at the mirror as she passed to check that her PJs were vaguely respectable. Her hair was a tousled mess. Her eyes looked too big for her face. She needed a shower, a hairbrush and some decent make-up.

She had time for none of them. Noah was waiting. She opened the door, Daisy launched herself up into his arms—a leap she was getting better and better at—and Noah was smiling right at her.

What was there in that to make a woman catch her breath? Honestly, she needed to get a grip.

'Good morning, Dr Blair.'

'G-good morning,' she managed. Then, a trifle defensively because he was standing there looking cool, collected and gorgeous and she was in her PJs, she added a rider. 'It's Sunday. People are allowed to sleep in on Sunday.'

'Unless it's a medical emergency.'

'Is there a medical emergency?' She couldn't see it in his body language.

'Sort of,' he said. 'I've decided you may be deficient in Vitamin D. It's therefore my job as your consultant surgeon to remedy that situation.'

'Since when have you been my consultant surgeon?'

'Am I a surgeon?'

'I… Yes.'

'And do you consult me for medical advice?'

'Of course, but—'

'Then I'm your consultant surgeon.' His smile widened. 'And Mrs Rowbotham, as our consultant housekeeper, concurs. There's nothing happening at the hospital that Rob can't cover. We still need to be within cooee, but that can be arranged. Daisy spent a very boring day yesterday and our consultant oldies…'

'Our consultant oldies?'

'We consult widely,' he said smoothly. 'The residents of Currawong Nursing Home agree. You have a unanimous diagnosis. Danger of Vitamin D level dropping. Dog boredom. And the prescription is simple. My backpack is therefore loaded with Mrs Rowbotham's finest culinary efforts. Also beach towels, sun screen, flippers, snorkels and masks. In case you hadn't noticed yet, the day is glorious, and we have a task in hand.'

She was struggling to get her head around what he was saying.

She was struggling to get her head around the way he was smiling at her.

'A…task?'

'Agate,' he said.

She blinked. 'Agate? What…?'

'Moonlight Bluff. You must know it.'

She did know Moonlight Bluff. She'd investigated when she'd first moved here. It was a strip of coastline a couple of miles south of the town, where the cliffs rose steeply to make the beach almost inaccessible. But there were steps down, steep and narrow, carved into the rock by some long-ago person with time on his hands, and skill. Once at the bottom you needed to wade into the cove where it was said you could find agate. If you were lucky.

'Did you know you can find agate there?' he said.

'I had heard that,' she conceded. 'At least… gemstones.'

'The agate's harder to find,' he conceded. 'The rocks have been pretty much picked over by centuries of fossickers. The word is that the best stones are to be found three quarters of the way up the steps when everyone's on their last gasp and ready to dump their loads just to get to the top. But I checked them out. They're okay, but nothing special.'

'Damned by faint praise.' She was feeling… totally disconcerted. She was still in her pyjamas.

He was still smiling at her.

'The locals make a fuss of them and who am I to argue? But, Addie, I've been diving around there…'

'Diving.'

'I swim,' he said, almost apologetically. 'The rock formations make diving a pleasure.'

'You carry your gear down those steps?'

'In my last life I was a mountain goat, bounding from peak to peak, so what's a few steps in this life? And once you're down it's magic. If you swim out around the headland the rock pools are stunning.' He paused as if a hiccup to his plans had suddenly interfered with his vision. 'You can swim?'

'I can.' Her response sounded ridiculously cautious.

'There you go, then. You're never more than a few metres from being able to stand up, and the sea today is mill-pond calm. And where I'm talking about… Agates, Addie. Black gold.'

'Black gold?' She was pretty much discombobulated.

'Okay, they're just gemstones,' he conceded. 'But they're beautiful. I saw them a few weeks ago. They're not everywhere but if you search the bottom at the far end of the cove you can find them. Tiny pieces of glossy black. Some have white lines, swirls, the most intricate patterns embedded. They're created by ancient volcanoes from liquefied silica. Agate's normally green, blue or amber. The black's rare and it's right on our doorstep.'

She was still confused but starting to be caught up in his enthusiasm. 'You found it.'

'I did.'

'But you didn't collect it?'

'Why would I?' He spread his hands. 'The

beach has mostly been picked clean and I had no reason to take any. But this morning...' His face changed again and suddenly he was serious.

'Addie, it's a special day,' he said softly. 'It's the morning after you discovered you were pregnant. You should have something to remember this weekend. I thought...if we could find a few stones, maybe we could have a stone set in a ring for you. And maybe we could make some into a bracelet or a signet ring for...for whoever might come along...'

She looked at his face. He was smiling again—sort of—but behind the smile she saw doubts. Fear?

Fear that she'd say no, that she'd walk inside and slam the door, closing him out from this pregnancy? This baby?

Closing him out from sharing, as he'd been shut off from Sophie?

This was his need, she thought. It wasn't hers, so that was okay.

Black agate... She'd seen it, polished to high lustre, and she'd seen stones with white hearts.

If they could find it...

'What do you think, Addie?' he asked, and she knew the decision was all hers.

'We could get back to the hospital in an emergency?'

'Rob and Cliff are covering for us, but we could. We'll take the car.'

'But all those steps…'

'I can carry you if necessary, yodelling at the same time. I told you, mountain goat fits my job description.'

'Do mountain goats yodel?' She choked on laughter, but then fell silent. He let her be while she formed an answer. As if he knew this decision was about more than stones.

This wasn't just about finding an agate or spending the day at the beach. This was about so much more…

Sharing.

They really should have some sort of relationship, she told herself. As long as it didn't involve need, it should be okay.

'I think,' she said at last, and finally she managed a smile, 'that Daisy and I would love it. And I also think…isn't it lucky I bought new bathers?'

* * *

Noah might describe himself as a mountain goat but Daisy outshone him. What obstacle was a hundred or so steps? The pup hared straight down, then up again, down and up, almost pleading with them to go faster.

But Noah was carrying a pack and he was walking with Addie. There was no way he was going faster.

Once upon a time he'd read that gentlemen should precede ladies down stairs, to catch them if they fell. It made sense, but Addie had headed down in front regardless. She seemed steady. She seemed safe. And if he'd been in front he couldn't have watched her bouncy curls, her gorgeous legs in her cute shorts, the way she stooped to hug Daisy whenever the pup reached them on one of her loops, the way Addie's body language said she was out to enjoy herself.

He thought of the day she'd returned to the hospital with her brand-new suitcase, her brand-new puppy and her brand-new attitude. She was a woman prepared to take on the world.

This pregnancy could knock it out of her. If something happened...

But nothing was happening today. Please.

They reached the base of the steps. Here was another reason why this place was generally deserted. The steps ended at a line of rocks, with no sand. To reach the cove itself you needed to wade around a rocky outcrop. But Addie obviously knew. She practically bounced down the last few steps, kicking off her sandals, then hauling off her T-shirt and shorts before she hit the water.

But not before he'd seen her bikini...

Of course it was a bikini—a New Version of Addie bikini. Skimpy, pert, bright crimson with white polka dots.

She beamed and stretched, holding her arms up as if to embrace the sun.

He believed he stopped. What man wouldn't have?

She took his breath away.

'Come on, slowcoach, the sea's waiting,' she called, and he gathered most of his wits and headed down the last few steps.

'Sunscreen,' he growled, because that was a

practical thing to say and a guy had to mask his emotions somehow.

'Already on,' she told him. 'I'm a woman prepared.' And then she hesitated and her smile grew almost teasing. 'Or usually prepared. Apart from one major slip-up.'

The pregnancy.

'Was it a slip-up?' he asked without thinking.

Her smile faded. 'You still suspect I planned things?' That was an out-of-character snap. 'It takes two to tango and it was just as much your fault as mine.' But then she shook her head. 'Nope. I'm not thinking that. It was no one's fault. A fault means dire consequences and right now there don't seem to be any dire consequences at all. I'm not even morning sick.'

'It's might be too early.'

'Don't you dare be a killjoy.' She was suddenly bossy. 'Let's get Daisy around to the cove. Then get your swimming gear on and hit the water. I'll see you in the deep end.'

And she lifted Daisy into her arms and headed into the shallows, wading around the rocks and leaving him to follow.

She'd dropped a sandal. He carried it with him, bemused.

By the time he'd rounded the rocks she'd dumped Daisy and her clothes on the sand. She'd adjusted a pair of prescription swimming goggles. Then she'd bounced through the minnow waves until a larger wave loomed close.

She flipped forward into a neat dive that told Noah she'd been swimming almost since before she could walk.

Daisy swam valiantly out to join her, but she was a smart pup. There were seagulls to chase and seaweed to sniff—and the sea was big. She headed back in.

And Noah was left…watching.

The sun was on his face. The cove was deserted and the sea was a sapphire dream, calling him to swim now.

Addie was treading water, waving. 'What's keeping you, slowcoach?'

He needed to catch his breath.

He took a couple of moments more, just to watch, as she started stroking strongly across the bay.

And then…

What's keeping you?
Nothing.

Addie was a fine swimmer. There'd been a public pool near her childhood home and she'd spent summer vacations enjoying it. She was therefore confident in the water, but Noah... Noah was something else. He dived into the oncoming waves and disappeared, the way a sleek seal would hunt for fish. When he appeared again he was further out, treading water, smiling.

And, oh, that smile...

'Race to warm up?' he demanded, and she had to catch her breath before she could answer.

'I saw you dive. I'm not dumb enough to race without a handicap,' she managed. 'So... To the side of the cove and back, ten times for you, seven for me.'

'Are you kidding? I watched you swim.'

'Eight, then,' she conceded. 'Ready, set, go.'

And she put her head down and swam, hard.

The water was clear and crystal clean. The bottom was sandy, with tiny fish darting out of their shadows. She'd normally be entranced.

She was…sort of entranced but maybe not by fish.

For a while she thought he'd beat her. He did three laps while she struggled to get two. But then he slowed.

Not because he was exhausted, though. He swam…with her? He dropped back to pace her, swimming alongside her with strong, easy strokes that told her he could go twice as fast if he wished.

He obviously didn't wish. After those first laps he matched himself to her. Every time her hand sliced the surface of the water, so did his. His body wasn't close enough to touch but close enough so she could feel the wash of him, so she was aware of him.

Entranced didn't begin to describe it.

She knew why she'd gone to bed with this man. It hadn't been a moment of madness. There was something about him… Some irresistible attraction…

It was almost as if…he was part of her?

Okay, that was a crazy thing to think and it wasn't exactly helpful, given the resolutions she'd made last night.

But a woman could fantasise…

A woman shouldn't, she told herself severely, trying to get her head to focus on her swimming. A woman would be very, very stupid to do any such thing.

But the matching of strokes was doing her head in.

She paused and trod water and Noah checked and did the same. 'Problem?'

'Just checking Daisy,' she told him, searching the shore. There was no need. Daisy was chasing seagulls, who seemed to have nothing better to do than to take off and land, over and over, forcing Daisy to run like a madcap.

'You just want a break,' Noah teased.

'Yeah, like there's a chance I might win if I cheat,' she retorted. 'I could double your handicap and still lose.'

'You wouldn't lose.' He smiled at her. 'Anyone less of a loser than you I have yet to meet.'

'Oh, *bleah*.' She shook her head in disgust. 'Did you get that out of some guy manual—lines for a pick-up? In case you've forgotten, the pick-up's already happened.'

'I didn't pick you up, Addie,' he said, smile

fading. 'You know that. And this is no seduc-
tion scene.'

'It feels like it.'

'You think I want to seduce you?'

'It might be the other way around,' she admitted, deciding she might as well be honest.
'And that…scares me.'

'There's no reason why it should.' And he
lifted his hand and touched her cheek.

She flinched.

Why? She wanted his touch. She knew she
did.

It did scare her, though.

Why?

Because it was for all the wrong reasons, she
told herself. He thought she needed him.

She would not be that woman. She shook her
head, flicking his hand away.

'Where are these agates?' she asked, more
roughly than she'd intended.

'So the race is off?' He was watching her.
Like a shark watched fish? Prey? Oh, for heav-
en's sake, she told herself, get a grip. This was
a nice guy, doing the right thing, with no hid-
den agenda. Yes, there was a bit of sexual at-

traction. It had gotten out of hand and there were consequences but that didn't mean it had to continue. Practical Addie was down there somewhere. She just had to dredge her up and send hormonal, wanting-to-jump-this-guy Addie back to where she'd come from.

Except she didn't actually know where hormonal Addie had come from. She'd been hiding...well, for most of her life. All her life?

She'd never felt like this with Gavin. Maybe there'd been a spark for her French teacher when she'd been twelve but who wouldn't have gone weak at the knees for a guy who spoke her name like it was the sexiest name in the world? Adeline in French...

She shivered and Noah was all concern. 'You're cold?'

'Nope. Just remembering...something I should have forgotten.' She gave herself a mental shake, relegating M'sieur Gauthier to obscurity, then attempted to do the same with Noah. It didn't quite work. 'Yes, the race is off,' she managed. 'Racing you is ridiculous. Show me where the agates are.'

She sounded brusque, even angry, but he

didn't seem to mind. He watched her for a moment, assessing?

She didn't like the way he looked at her. Or maybe she did but it had her totally… discombobulated? She felt twelve years old all over again, ready to stammer over her French primer.

'You need to swim around the rocks on this side,' he told her. 'It's deep water but at the far side there's a shelf where the agates seem to have collected. It's only about two metres deep.'

'I can dive that far,' Addie told him, and turned away to swim.

Two metres?

She was already way out of her depth.

Finding the perfect agate was a laborious business, because Noah was fussy.

He was right in that there were plenty of stones. He dived and spent a little time choosing before bringing a few special ones to the surface for inspection. Addie wasn't as good at staying under water. She dived, grab a handful of whatever she could grab, then dumped them on a rock ledge to sort, while Noah dived some more.

It was disconcerting, holding onto the ledge, sorting stones, while Noah dived underneath her.

It was more than disconcerting, though. She had to concede that it felt good. Or more than good. Gorgeous?

The sun was on her face. The water was cool and lovely. Daisy had discovered she could reach their ledge by clambering over the rocks, so she had a puppy in her face helping her sort.

Noah was diving like the seal he was, bringing up stones for her inspection.

And the stones needed very careful inspection. She didn't need to dive again with Noah.

She was scared to?

Oh, for heaven's sake…

She sorted and Noah dived until he was sure he had enough to check himself. Finally he heaved himself up onto the ledge.

He was wearing boxers. Nothing else. Lean, muscled, tanned…dark hair dripping water across his face…

She was still in the water, holding the ledge

with one hand while she sorted with the other. He was right above her.

M'sieur Gauthier was relegated to even more obscurity.

'What have we got?' he asked, checking the pile, and she thought, trouble, that's what she had, but somehow she made herself answer.

'I think…there are some good ones… We could sort them back at the beach.'

'Let's do it here,' he said. 'We only need one or two. We should drop the rest back where they came from so some other couple needing special stones can find them.'

Couple…

Yeah, okay, her mind was ditzy. One word should not make her feel like this.

She didn't answer. She focussed on stones and after a moment's silence—a moment where the word *couple* seemed to hang over them— so did Noah.

The stones Noah selected were small, pea- to marble-sized, deep black with white flecks. They'd been smoothed by years of rolling in the surf, glossy when wet but already losing their gloss as they dried.

'They'll come up magnificently when they're tumbled,' he said, picking up a small stone, wetting it again and holding it to the light. 'This one… Look at the depth of the black and the purity of the white. But the white forms a line, almost a division. I'm looking for a white heart.'

'Tumbled?' she queried. She sort of knew what tumbling stones involved but it was easier than following the other line of thought. Hearts…

Why was everything getting away from her? This was a morning spent collecting precious stones. Why make it something it wasn't?

'My grandpa used to collect gemstones,' he told her. 'He had a tumbler. I remember being awed at the way the stones were transformed. Now I'm not going to London…' he abandoned the stone he was checking and picked up another '…maybe I could buy me a tumbler.'

'But… If you don't get custody of Sophie, you need to go to London.'

'Why?'

'Because that's what you planned.'

'Nope,' he said easily. 'I planned on getting

away. I planned on changing my life. Somehow that's already happened.'

'Noah, I won't be responsible for—'

'You're responsible for nothing, Addie,' he told her, suddenly firm. 'I'm a grown man and I make my own decisions. Staying in Australia? Buying a tumbler?' He hesitated. He glanced down at her and she saw the flash of sudden uncertainty. Vulnerability?

'Maybe even falling in love?' he added, so quietly that for a moment she thought she must have misheard.

She hadn't, though. The tiny waves washed in and out of the cove. Daisy rushed across and pounced on the pile of discarded stones, then rushed away again.

The words stayed where they were.

Falling in love?

'No.' She said it flatly. It was as if there was a shield somewhere within her that had to be raised. It was heavy, cumbersome, hard to raise but somehow she managed it.

'Why not? Other people do.'

'You wouldn't say it if I wasn't pregnant. If you didn't think I needed you.'

'You don't think I might say it despite the fact that you're pregnant?' He tucked a wet curl back from her eyes, setting it behind her ear. He did it with surgical precision, as if it was infinitely important that the curl be set just so. 'You're adorable, Addie.'

'Daisy's adorable.' She was having trouble catching her breath.

'So she is, but she's not someone I'd choose to marry.'

Marry.

Memories flooded back like a tsunami, the months, no, years, of planning the wedding of the century, her mother's joy, the culmination of the interminable car journey to church. And then... Her mother's pain. Gavin's mum's pain. No one knowing what to say. Standing in the sunshine in her stupid white tulle, dropping her overblown bouquet at her feet, knowing she looked ridiculous, hating Gavin with every fibre of her being, Gavin who, minutes before, she'd thought was her best friend...

Gavin, who'd accused her...of needing him.

'You really think that's what I'd want?' she whispered, appalled. 'Marriage?'

'Um…possibly not,' he said ruefully. 'Can you forget I said it? It was a stupid thing to say and it's scared us both. Marriage doesn't have to come into it. Not for a long, long time, maybe not for ever. But love… Addie, maybe we could concede it's possible. I know it's too soon but…'

'Both of us have tried before.' Her voice was hard. The armour was finally raised, hammered into place by shock and fear. 'Both of us know it's a disaster. Love comes with strings that break your heart. I don't need it.'

'Are we talking about need, or talking about love?'

'They work the same. I can't take the chance…'

'I'm not asking you to take a chance.' He was starting to sound exasperated. 'I'm asking you to drop your barriers for a bit because all they do is hurt. I'm asking to get to know you better. I want to see what makes you laugh, makes you cry. I want to learn what you like on your toast. I want to see you as I did this morning, rumpled, real. I've seen so many Addies…'

'Yeah, the white tulle…'

'And the workhorse Addie, and the frightened

patient Addie, and the Daisy-toting, luggage-kicking Addie. And the Addie who lay in my arms. And, this morning, the rumpled, gorgeous Addie. And now the dripping, beautiful woman who won't get out of the water and sit beside me because she's afraid...'

'I'm not afraid.'

'Liar.'

'Okay, I am.' It was a yell, so unexpected that Daisy stopped dead in her quest to catch a seagull, and headed over the rocks at full pace to see what was wrong.

Only when she reached them she looked from Addie—still two-thirds in the water—and Noah, and made her choice. She shoved her nose under Noah's arm and made her allegiance clear.

'Traitor.' Addie hauled back on her fright—yes, okay, she was frightened—and summoned reserves to haul herself from the water. Noah put out a hand to help but she simply glared at it.

Did he smile? The toe rag. He'd better not be laughing.

'We have enough stones,' she said with an attempt at dignity. 'I believe it's time to go home.'

'Mrs Rowbotham's made us lunch. It's in the backpack.'

'I don't want any.'

'Addie?'

'Yes?' She hauled herself up, standing, dripping water on the rock beside him. It felt better standing up. Safer.

'You don't think you might be being a bit melodramatic? We haven't made a final choice of stones, and lunch needs to be eaten.'

'Yeah, okay,' she muttered. 'Just don't say the L word again.'

'Love?'

'Noah!' Drat it, he really was laughing.

'Okay.' He held his hands up in surrender. 'No L word. Or even what seems to be more scary. The N word. Need. For now all talk of future relationship is off the table. But we still need to be colleagues. Daisy needs us to be friends and, who knows, we might need to co-parent one day. So let's start being civilised about it. Lunch and stone sorting and maybe a wee nap in the sun before we head home.'

'Okay,' she said grudgingly, and then, because she really had sounded grumpy and it was a gorgeous day and he was a friend, she tried harder. 'Sorry. You gave me a fright but I'm over it. Lunch, stone sorting but a nap's out of the question. New limits.'

'Accepted,' he said, and gathered the remaining stones and stood.

He was large. He was still wet. He was...

Don't go there. New limits. Lunch, stones and no nap.

Starting now.

Except she did nap and Noah was left staring out to sea wondering what he'd just said.

The L word.

What had he been thinking?

He suspected Addie had gone to sleep thinking he'd spoken in order to gain access to a child who was finally his. It was a reasonable thought. She knew he loved Sophie and might lose her. She'd guess now that he'd love this baby, too.

But what he felt for Addie was different. Far different.

Maybe she couldn't see it because almost every time he'd seen her she'd been at her most vulnerable. He couldn't deny it, but when the chips were down, that was when you saw the real person. The slap at the wedding. Her courage and fear in the face of an ectopic pregnancy. Her defiance and bounce as she'd returned, with a puppy and bright red luggage…

And a polka-dot bikini. She was wearing a crimson sarong now as she slept, but the polka-dot top peeped out. Her damp curls were splayed across her towel-cum-pillow. Her glasses were clutched in her hand. Her glasses were almost a line of defence, he thought. She could be awake and wary in seconds.

Wary of him?

Wary of talk of love? Of mutual need?

Was she right? Was it dumb talk?

Maybe it was, but it was the way she made him feel. She was vulnerable and needful but she was also feisty, skilled and strong. Fun.

To walk away from her now seemed unthinkable.

If this baby happened, she'd give him access. He knew it, but he wasn't thinking of a baby.

He was watching a woman sleep. *His woman. Part of him?* The sense of oneness was so deep, so primeval it almost left him gasping. After Rebecca…the thought of another relationship had seemed unthinkable, but somehow, some way, Addie had breached defences he'd hardly known he had.

So… How to convince her to take a chance on more than friendship?

It wasn't something she could be 'convinced' of, he thought. It was simply the way things were—or weren't. If she didn't feel it, that was that. He was the last person to try and force such an issue.

So back away, he told himself. You're scaring her. Be a friend and take the pressure off. Like now. Go for another swim rather than sit and stare like a stalker.

But he wanted to sit. To guard his woman?

How corny was that?

He rose and headed for the water again, though Daisy looked up as he left and whimpered a reproach.

Your place is here with us, her whimper seemed to say, but he knew it wasn't.

But if not…he didn't have a clue where his place was.

Addie didn't…wouldn't…need him and the thought left him bleak.

He dived under a wave and stayed under for a very long time.

CHAPTER ELEVEN

THE PREGNANCY WASN'T ECTOPIC. The pregnancy was safe in utero. Blood tests promised it. A scan at five weeks confirmed it.

She told Noah at the end of long day's surgery. She watched his face light up. She backed away as he went to hug her, and she went back to her cottage.

And closed the door.

Honestly? She was too frightened to do anything else. The thought of him falling in love... Of *her* falling in love...was terrifying. All the control she'd so carefully cultivated seemed to be as threatened as a house of cards in a wind storm.

As the weeks wore on, they settled into an uneasy pattern. Friends? Colleagues? Outwardly they were just that. And maybe it was true, she thought as she worked on. Noah was certainly respecting her boundaries. They worked together. They met in the staffroom and talked about shared patients, about dog training, about ordinary stuff. He shared some of her dog walking. He was friendly, warm... normal?

And yet there was part of her that knew that he was contained. Holding things back.

The phrase he'd used on the beach...*falling in love*...stayed with her. She woke in the night and it was there. She met him in the corridor and it was there. She saw him below the hospital, throwing a Frisbee for Daisy, and it was there.

Love?

It was crazy, she thought. How could anyone fall in love so fast? The way he felt *must* be all to do with the baby. His relationship with her... He thought she needed him and he was honourable. How could it be more than that?

She should block out the emotion, but as the weeks went on another layer came into play.

It was getting closer to his court hearing for custody of Sophie. She saw him occasionally out on the veranda, taking long calls, and his face was always set and grim.

It was nothing to do with her, so why did her heart twist for him?

Her thoughts were all over the place.

She wanted to share his pain. If they were friends that's what she'd do, she thought, but the emotions he caused had her backing away.

Falling in love...

Impossible.

She moved from day to day, trying to block his unsettling presence. Trying to focus on her work and her pregnancy.

Her baby.

His baby.

How would co-parenting work? As her baby's father, he'd be in her life...for ever?

But just as her baby's father.

She'd worry about that when she had to, she told herself. Even though the pregnancy was where it was supposed to be, she was still barely allowing herself to hope.

She'd manage as she'd always managed.

She did not need Noah.

Fourteen weeks...

Not that he was counting. Not much. But this was Addie's pregnancy and he had to back off.

Eventually he wanted to be a part of this child's life. He knew enough of Addie not to fear being shut out, but shutting him out of his child's life was different to shutting him out of hers.

And that's what she'd done. It was her right, but still he counted.

Fourteen weeks…

And two more weeks until the family court case for Sophie. That was doing his head in.

If anything happened to Addie's baby… If anything happened to Addie… If he lost the court case as his lawyers told him he probably would… If he lost the right to see Sophie…

And then one morning he had a phone call.

He took it, and couldn't believe what he was hearing. He disconnected, then stared sightlessly out to sea while his world changed. And when it settled…

For some reason there was only one thing he could think of to do.

Sadly medicine had to come first, but he could deal with that.

He had two more patients to see before he could go tell Addie.

* * *

At fourteen weeks she'd finally booked in for the scan most pregnant women had at twelve weeks. She'd been…sort of scared to do it? The twelve-week scan would show arms, legs, a little face. Or not. It seemed like she was tempting fate to take the scan and find out.

At fourteen weeks she could put it off no longer but her scheduled appointment had to be set back. The radiologist who came to Currawong once a week was running late.

Addie headed into the staffroom. She made herself tea, put her head on her hands for a moment and closed her eyes…

'Dr Blair!'

She woke and Morvena was standing over her, looking astonished. Her tea was cooling in front of her.

She'd been fast asleep.

'What…?' It took a moment to collect herself. 'Sorry. Just…catching up with a quick nap between patients.' She checked her watch and relaxed. She had ten more minutes before she was due in Radiology.

But Morvena was still staring at her, and

Addie could see calculations going on in her head. Fast calculations.

Uh-oh.

'There were no babies born last night,' Morvena said. 'No call-outs.' If anyone knew this, it was Morvena who had a finger on the pulse of the whole hospital. 'Why do you need to catch up on sleep?'

'I just…didn't sleep last night.'

'The lights were out in your cottage. All night.'

Honestly, was there anything this woman didn't know? Addie decided it wasn't worth a response. She rose and carried her mug to the sink, busying herself washing it. With her back to Morvena.

But she knew, reply or not, she was faced with the inevitable.

And here it came. 'You're pregnant again, aren't you?'

Go away, Addie wanted to say. This is nobody's business—nobody's baby—but mine. Admitting it to an outsider seemed fraught. Everything seemed fraught.

The scan just minutes away seemed terrifying, and now this…

She set her cleaned mug on the bench and held her hands to her tummy. She refused to turn around. She was holding her baby to herself. Holding hope.

'It's Dr McPherson's,' Morvena said.

It wasn't a question.

That took her breath away. She counted to ten, not because she needed to control what she was going to say but because she couldn't think of what to say.

'Leave it, Morvena,' she managed at last. 'Dr McPherson's due to leave in two weeks. It's hardly helpful to start rumours now.'

'I'm starting no rumours,' Morvena retorted. 'I'm stating facts. He's looking grim as death. You're falling asleep all over the hospital. I'm losing an excellent surgeon and I have an obstetrician who can't keep her eyes open. If that's not my business I don't know what is.'

'I'm fourteen weeks. I should be getting over fatigue soon.'

Oh, for heaven's sake, why had she said that? She should have denied it. Morvena had quizzed her before about the paternity of her ectopic pregnancy and she'd admitted the IVF treatment. She should have implied it was more of the same.

But it was too late now. Morvena's eyes narrowed. 'Fourteen weeks...' She could see her doing mental arithmetic and finding the answer. 'I'm right, then. And you moved out of the doctors' house because...'

'Because it was a mistake. Because neither of us want—'

'Well, that's nonsense,' Morvena said briskly. 'You both want. Here you are, buying a dog that distracts the running of the entire hospital, when what you want is home and hearth and babies. And so does he.'

'Morvena, I don't. We don't—'

'Nonsense. I've seen the way you look at him. And the way he looks at you.'

'He has enough on his plate. Do you know—?' She broke off, aghast. The court case was definitely not for public consumption.

'About his little girl? Of course I know. And not because I snoop,' Morvena said briskly. 'He takes phone calls at the end of the veranda, and my office is just through the window. I acknowledge I shouldn't know, but I'm not stupid. I know why he's looking grim. I also know why he's looking at you like he is.'

'Morvena, enough.' She didn't know whether to laugh or cry. She glanced at her watch. 'I need to be in Radiology in five minutes.'

'For your own appointment. I saw.'

'You have no right—'

'I have every right. It's part of my job to check Frieda's appointments. If no one's booked in, it's my job to tell her not to come. When I saw your name I worried it was for something serious. Until I thought about it a bit more.'

'Morvena...'

And then, amazingly the woman softened. 'It's okay, my dear,' she told her. 'I'm not about to shout it abroad. So you're off to have a fourteen-week scan. Is Noah going with you?'

'I... No.'

'You haven't told him you're having the scan?'

'It's nothing to do with him.'

'Why on earth not?'

'Because it can't be.' It was practically a wail, and suddenly it was as if a dam broke. 'Morvena, what if I'm in love with him? I won't let him take care of me because I need him. I won't. We've both been in relationships like that and it scares me stupid.'

Whoa.

How much had she exposed? What had she just said?

And to whom? Because suddenly…it wasn't just Morvena.

She stared blindly at the nurse manager, but as panic receded she became aware of a shadow behind. Blocking the doorway.

Noah.

What had he just heard? Beam me up, Scotty, she pleaded with the universe. Where was a time machine when she needed one?

'You know,' Morvena said, quite conversationally, 'I just remembered there's a rumour about a puppy in the kids' ward. If you'll excuse me, I have rules to enforce.' And she had the temerity to grin. 'Dr McPherson, I believe you have sense to enforce things as well. This woman's in love with you even if she won't admit it. Anyone who tells someone as grouchy as me that they might be in love…well, once upon a time I was foolish as well, and it got me a loving husband and a couple of children who are just as foolish as their mother was. Sometimes foolish is altogether sensible. I'll leave you both to it.'

And she had the effrontery to chuckle, a sound almost unheard of from Morvena, as she bustled away to do her duty.

Leaving Addie with Noah.

How long had he been there?

'I… Is Daisy…?' She was struggling to breathe, much less talk. Her fast-growing pup seemed the safest—the only option. 'Is Daisy in the kids' ward?'

'Daisy might have been in the kids' ward,' Noah said, his voice carefully neutral. 'I believe she might now be in Men's Surgical.' By rights Daisy should be in her playpen but increasingly the friendly pup was 'borrowed' at need. Keeping her out of the wards was a task even Morvena seemed to be giving up on.

'I… I have to go,' Addie tried.

'To have your ultrasound.'

'How long were you standing there?'

'Long enough. Sound carries down corridors and Morvena's never been one to lower her voice.'

'I…'

'Addie, would you like me to come?'

And it was exactly the wrong question. Or the right question?

Would you like me to come? No pressure.

All the pressure in the world.

If he'd said *I want to come*, she'd have handled that. But would she *like*?

'I don't need—' she managed.

'Let's leave need out of it,' he said, his voice suddenly rough with emotion. 'Let's focus on what we want. Addie, you're about to have an ultrasound that is important. Fourteen weeks… It'll tell you if there are any problems you need to face—that *we* need to face. More probably, it'll tell us that we have a healthy, normal baby settling down to grow for the next two trimesters. I would like to be there. No, I want to be there. There's no need involved, only desire. But you're right, we've both been pushed in directions that weren't our choice and I won't do that to you. I will not. So trust me or not, this is the time to say it. What do you want?'

What did she want?

She wanted her baby. That was her one inviolate truth. Her hands were still on her belly, as if she could protect that truth from any outside threats simply by holding.

Was Noah a threat?

Somehow she'd made him out to be, but he was standing in front of her now and she looked into his face and what she saw…

It was just… Noah.

A colleague.

A friend.

An honourable man.

A man who'd held her and made the outside world disappear.

A man who could love her baby as much as she did. She knew that.

A man who could love her?

It was too soon to think that. Panic was still there, rearing its ugly head in the background. To let go…

But she didn't need to let go. Not completely. All he was asking was to say what she wanted right now.

Did she want him to be with her at the ultrasound?

The scan she'd had at five weeks had shown nothing except the position of the pregnancy. Her baby had been the size of an apple seed. She had a chart of baby growth versus fruit sizes that she showed her pregnant mums. They liked it and so did she.

At this scan her baby should be the size of a lemon. Or a peach? Peach, she thought. She liked the image.

An image…

She'd see it. At fourteen weeks her baby could be sucking a thumb, wiggling toes. It'd be real. If everything was okay…

If something was wrong, could she bear it? Even now, the fear was still with her.

Did she want Noah with her?

And the answer came back, as clear as day. Yes, she did.

And more.

She didn't want him because she needed a support person. She didn't…need.

She wanted him because she knew he wanted

this baby as much as she did. This baby meant love to Noah as well.

Love...

It was a concept she was having trouble getting her head around, but it was present, somewhere in this utilitarian staffroom with its noisy refrigerator and uncomfortable chairs and its unwashed coffee mugs. Mrs Rowbotham was always having forty fits about medics who grabbed coffee on the run and didn't clean up.

She'd cleaned hers, she thought inconsequentially.

Love...

Noah was waiting. Calmly. Whatever she said, he wouldn't push.

Did she want him to be there for the ultrasound? Did she want him to share?

'Yes, please,' she whispered, and then, more loudly, 'Noah, yes, please, I'd love you to come.'

Normal was a strange word. It sounded dull, plain. It didn't begin to describe how she felt as she lay and let the ultrasound wand stroke her belly.

Normal?

It was a fabulous word.

Frieda was talking them through what she was seeing, obviously enjoying their wonder.

'I'm counting vertebrae. Every single one in place. Gorgeously normal. Head circumference…within normal limits. Great. Head down, beautiful presentation, though there's lots of time to wiggle. Now sex… You know at fourteen weeks it's hard. I've seen a lot of ultrasounds and I could hazard a guess but—'

'No.' The word came from both of them at exactly the same time. Addie looked up at Noah and he looked down at her and then they both looked at the screen. And Noah's hand suddenly slipped into hers and gripped, hard.

She lay and watched the faint movement on the screen. Her baby—*their* baby—was trying to kick. And Addie was grinning like the proverbial Cheshire Cat, grinning and grinning because who couldn't grin in the face of such joy?

Normal.

What was normal about a perfect baby?

What was normal about a guy holding her hand? Her baby's father.

Noah.

Sharing her joy.

'I'll write the results up, but everything's wonderful,' Frieda was saying, and Addie thought 'wonderful' was an even better word than 'normal'. Or maybe they were the same. 'Would you like a print of the image? Or I could copy the file and send it to you.'

'Yes,' they said again, once more totally in unison, and Noah chuckled and Addie found herself doing exactly the same. Frieda was wiping lubricant from her belly. The scan was done.

Time to release Noah's hand?

No. And that was a unilateral decision as well.

His grip firmed. He helped her to sit up, then moved in to hug and Frieda had to manoeuvre past him.

'I do love a happy ending,' Frieda said. 'Or a happy beginning. Welcome to your second trimester, Dr Blair, Dr McPherson and baby.'

And that felt great, too.

Maybe all parents felt like this. Maybe this was normal?

Normal.

She was getting to love that word. If the feel of Noah's hand in hers could be…normal…

It was still too soon, she told herself, a trace of fear rearing its ugly head, so she didn't say it. But as she dressed, as Noah opened the door to the outside world, he took her hand in his again and she thought…

Normal could be just plain awesome.

But the outside world was waiting.

She was floating in a bubble of euphoria but the moment they emerged she felt Noah stiffen.

The X-ray department had two entrances, a door leading back into the hospital and another for outpatients, opening to the veranda. They'd emerged to the veranda because why wouldn't they? The sun was shining, the sea was sapphire and sparkling to the horizon, and the world was waiting.

But something else was waiting.

A car had just pulled into the staff car park, a white sedan with government number plates. A middle-aged woman, dressed in a smart black business suit, was emerging from the driver's seat.

She opened a rear door and helped a child out. A little girl dressed in blue dungarees and crimson trainers. She had deep black hair, tied into two pigtails with red-checked ribbon. Her face was broad, her big round eyes looking cautiously out to see where she was.

And even from the veranda, Addie could tell...

Sophie.

She knew even before Noah dropped her hand and strode—and then ran—down the steps, across the car park, to scoop the little girl into his arms. She knew, even before the little girl clung, her little arms going around his neck, her face burrowing into his shoulder.

'Papa...' the child said, wonderingly, and something very like a sob broke from Noah. His face was in her hair. He was holding her like she was the most precious thing in the world. Just holding.

Love... The word was all around them.

This child wasn't Noah's, Addie thought,

dazed. This was Rebecca's child, foisted on him…

No, not foisted. He'd taken her willingly, more than willingly.

Because she needed him?

No. There was nothing even close to obligation on Noah's face. There was only joy.

He turned with the little girl in his arms. He smiled across at Addie and she saw the glimmer of tears on his face.

She still wasn't sure what was going on. There was an official Government Family Services logo on the car. The woman—a social worker?—was standing back, smiling, but she was holding a clipboard. Official business?

'Sophie, this is my friend, Addie,' Noah told the little girl, and the child gave her a long, considering stare before burying her face in Noah's shoulder again. Noah kissed the top of her head and then turned back to the woman by the car.

'Thank you,' he said, and there was such fervency in the words that Addie could only wonder.

'I'll leave you to it,' she ventured, increasingly unsure of her place. 'I… I have patients to see.'

'Wait,' Noah said. 'Addie, this is important. Stay for a moment. Can you come and meet Sophie?'

So she allowed her legs to carry her down the steps, to where Noah stood hugging his little girl, while the woman in the suit beamed her approval in the background.

'Addie, this is my Sophie,' Noah told her. But as Sophie kept her face in his shoulder, he smiled and turned to the lady with the clipboard. 'And this is Dianne, Sophie's social worker. And risk taker and miracle worker.'

'Wow,' Addie managed, and was offered a hand in greeting and took it. 'That's some recommendation.'

'She deserves it and more,' Noah told her. 'She's won me my Sophie.'

'I don't understand.' There was a lot she didn't understand. The depth of her lack of understanding was bottomless.

'Sophie's foster father had a heart attack last week.' Noah was still hugging Sophie, talking over her head, speaking softly so he wouldn't startle her. 'Her foster mother has been by his bedside ever since. There are no short-term carers available right now. I'm not permitted access, so Sophie had to go into a group home. She went into meltdown. As her case worker, Dianne had to make the arrangements but she hated seeing how confused and upset Sophie was. And she also knew I was here, loving Sophie, adoption papers lodged, court case pending, aching for access.'

'It was exceedingly unsatisfactory.' The social worker spoke briskly, holding her clipboard before her as if to make everything business-like. 'Noah's been acting as much as a father as he's been permitted to for five years. We know he wants custody. He ticks every box as far as suitability goes, yet Sophie's mother has the rights. It was frustrating everyone, and when her foster arrangements fell through it became a crisis.'

'I can't bear to think…' Noah said, and his voice cracked.

'It was only for a week,' Dianne said soothingly, seeing the emotion on Noah's face. 'But things did become untenable. Sophie was disintegrating at the group home, withdrawn, not eating, sobbing her heart out, and there seemed nothing we could do. We're well overstretched in the department but finally I...*we*...took the time to go through her case notes since birth. I only joined the department eighteen months ago so a lot of it was new to me, but I realised there were inconsistencies between Rebecca's statements as to her ability to care for her, and Rebecca's obvious ability to function in the community. I made...subtle enquiries and exposed Rebecca's miscommunication. Finally the question solidified. Why don't we simply take her back to her mother?'

'Because Rebecca hates her?' Noah said, softly though, his hand ruffling the little girl's hair to muffle her hearing.

'Be that as it may,' Dianne said primly. 'Rebecca's never admitted that. Her case for fostering was based on the extent of her disability, which I believe I've proved to be less than she's previously implied. Our job then was to make an immediate call on how to get Sophie out of a situation where she was clearly failing. Once we had the facts we called a case conference to decide whether Sophie could be returned to her mother's care. There's never been any hint that Sophie had been mistreated by Rebecca. We decided we could keep constant supervision and that we could pull her out at need. So we rang Rebecca and said we were bringing her home to her—immediately.'

'I can only imagine how that went down,' Noah said with feeling, and Dianne gave a tight smile.

'The child's welfare is paramount. We had no choice. We knew that Rebecca was living with a new partner—we'd done background checks on him before the case conference. There was no hint he was unfit for the placement but it seems *he* didn't know of Sophie's existence. Maybe that would have been a deal breaker in their relationship—Rebecca's reaction seemed to suggest that. Her first reaction was fury, then denial—and then panic.'

'Of course panic,' Noah said, hugging Sophie tighter.

'I admit we were concerned,' the social worker told them. 'We were ready to back off.

But we hung on long enough for Rebecca to panic herself into another way.'

She gave a slightly shamefaced smile then, a crack in the professional façade. 'And that was our success. It was the way I, *we*…had hoped. Rebecca was searching wildly for any way out and Noah was the only short-term alternative we gave her.' Once again that embarrassed smile. 'It may have been slightly unprofessional in pushing at this time, but by the end of the phone call the objection to Noah's adoption had been dropped. The papers were signed the next morning, while her new partner was at golf. The only stipulation is that Noah remains quiet about Sophie's parentage. Sophie will have that information from us when and if she needs it. Of course there'll be further formalities, but as far as we can tell there'll be no further problems.'

'And you have my undying gratitude,' Noah said, and then he couldn't say any more. His face was buried in Sophie's hair. He was just… holding.

Dianne and Addie looked at the little girl, clinging like a wee limpet. Dianne smiled but

Addie couldn't even bring herself to smile. There was a lump in her throat so big she was struggling to breathe.

He wanted this little girl.

But Sophie wasn't his child. There was no need for him to get involved. There'd never been a need.

He loved her.

Love…

The word was all around her, singing its way into her heart.

Love.

Dianne was taking gear out of the car. Sophie was lifting her head from Noah's shoulder, looking around with caution at this new world she'd just been introduced to.

Noah met her gaze over Sophie's head and he smiled and smiled.

It was too much. Tears were sliding down her face and she couldn't check them.

'I… Excuse me,' she managed. 'I have… I have patients booked. I'll…'

She could think of nothing else to say.

She turned and fled back into the hospital.

But love stayed with her. Noah's smile. Dianne's triumph. The way Sophie clung.

More. The events of the morning were overwhelming. The grainy pictures on an ultrasound.

She needed Daisy, she decided. Where was
a puppy when she needed one?

'Which room *isn't* Daisy in at the moment?'
she asked Heidi as she met her in the corridor,
and Heidi looked at her in concern.

'Is everything okay?'

'I… Yes… I just…need Daisy.'

'Daisy might currently *not* be in Room
Seven,' Heidi told her. 'But—'

'Thanks,' she said, cutting off further questions. She headed for Room Seven and found
one half-grown retriever puppy entertaining an
elderly woman recovering from a fall.

'Hi, Mrs Crammond. Do you mind if I bor-
row my dog? I sort of…need her.'

'Of course you do.' Mrs Crammond beamed
as Daisy scrambled off the bed and headed for
her mistress. 'Everyone needs a puppy to hug.'

'Everyone needs a hug,' Addie concurred, and
then added a rider. 'Everyone needs…love?'

CHAPTER TWELVE

IT WAS EIGHT at night.

Addie had worked through, seeing one patient after another, and then organised a house call to a woman she suspected was at risk of postnatal depression. There was probably no need to go this evening, but it was on her list of things to do and she needed things to do.

She took Daisy with her. She sat at the woman's kitchen table and admired her new baby as she talked with her and her husband. She talked about how hard it was to adjust to parenting, to the demands of a totally different life. She talked about the lack of structure, of sleep deprivation, of fears of the future.

Addie talked of strategies. Of a plan, with sleep rosters starting that night. She helped a self-contained, controlled woman explore the idea that she needed to let go, to ask for help, to not have everything perfect.

She left them cautiously hopeful, facing challenges together.

Together was a good word.

She couldn't get it out of her head.

She drove back to her cottage, had tea and toast, tucked Daisy into her bed and then walked across to the doctors' house.

The word was still ringing in her ears.

Together.

Noah was sitting on the veranda step.

She'd known he would be. She'd just known.

Because she knew this man?

Because she loved him.

He didn't get up as she approached. He had a beer in his hand. He put it down but went no further.

The night was totally, absolutely still. Or maybe it wasn't. She could hear the gentle hush of waves washing in and out on the beach below. She could hear the call of curlews, but nothing else. The world seemed at peace.

Waiting?

'I came to ask…' she said, and stopped. How to say it? How to take this giant leap?

He didn't help. How could he? she thought.

He'd given her so much. The control had all been hers.

He would never push, not this man. A man who'd taken on the care of a child who wasn't his. A man who'd entered a loveless marriage because how could he not?

A man who'd said the love word to her and seen her back away in fright.

'I came to ask if you'd marry me,' she said.

Silence.

The silence was so deep it was terrifying. The curlews had stopped their calling. Even the waves seemed to have stilled.

Had she got it so wrong?

'Why?' he asked at last, and his voice didn't seem like his. It was distant. Faint. As if he, too, was facing a barrier he'd never contemplated crossing.

But there was only one answer and she had to say it. Out loud. Right there and then.

'Because I love you,' she said.

More silence. Neither of them seemed able to move. He was still seated on the top step. She was a metre or so from the bottom step, looking up at him.

Holding her breath.

The whole world seemed to be holding its breath.

'I don't need you,' he said at last.

It could have been a rejection but it wasn't. She knew this man. She knew what he was saying.

'I don't need you either,' she told him. 'I can manage by myself and so can you. I can also give you any access to our baby that you want. We can co-parent without marriage. And you… Noah, I know you'll be a beautiful dad to Sophie without any help from me. So I don't need you and you don't need me. But today… It's taken me a while to figure it out but when I saw your face as you held Sophie… When I saw how much you loved… Noah, I'd love to share. I'd love…to love, too. If you'd let me…'

He stood then, but still he didn't come to her. She saw his face under the dim veranda light and she saw the wash of emotion.

'Sophie…' he said slowly, as if struggling to emerge from a dream. 'Sometimes… Addie, sometimes she's not easy.'

And there was only one answer to that. She

said what was in her heart. What she truly believed. 'She'll be our daughter,' she said, and had to force her voice to rise above a whisper. 'Our family. Noah, I'm not asking for easy. I want it all. If you'll let me.'

'The full bells and whistles…'

'Not quite,' she admitted. 'Marriage with you? Yes and yes and yes. Co-parenting Sophie and my bump and a crazy pup called Daisy? Yes, please, to that, too. But Noah, I won't wear white tulle again. Not even for you.'

'Not even a little bit?' He sounded so forlorn she had to chuckle, but a girl had to set limits somewhere.

'Not even a little bit,' she told him. 'I've sworn off the stuff for life. Noah…' She took a deep breath. 'The marriage thing…what do you reckon?'

And he smiled.

He smiled and he smiled, and his smile finally, finally carried him down the steps. Slowly, as if he couldn't believe what was waiting for him below.

Finally he reached her. He took her hands in his and he searched her face.

'You're sure, my Addie.'

'I love you, Noah.'

'And I love you,' he told her. 'If you'll do me the honour of becoming my wife, I'll be the happiest man alive.'

'But…you wouldn't be marrying because of need.' She was still anxious.

'See, there's the thing,' he said, almost ruefully. 'I would be. It's been a while now since I conceded that I need you. But it's you I need, Addie. Not anything you can do for me or mine. I just need…you.'

'Then I guess I need you,' she admitted, and as she said it something inside her seemed to crack. To melt. To disappear as if it had never been.

Years of building armour. Years of doing the right thing. Years of emptiness. They'd disappeared to nothing.

There was no emptiness now. Noah was looking into her eyes with such love, with such want, with such need…

Maybe need was a good word, she thought, and then, as Noah dropped to one knee she decided it was the best word she'd ever heard.

'Then let's do it properly,' Noah said, his voice husky with passion. 'Adeline Margaret Blair, will you do me the very great honour of becoming my wife?'

'How do you know my middle name?' she asked, weirdly sidetracked, and his gorgeous smile widened.

'I looked it up on staff records…just in case I ever needed it.'

She chuckled and she, too, dropped to one knee. 'Me, too,' she admitted. 'I sort of… needed the whole box and dice. So… Noah William McPherson, yes, please,' she whispered. 'And will you…?'

'Don't be daft, love,' he told her and his arms drew her into him. Firmly. Strongly. 'You've already asked. But, yes, please, too.'

And then there was no need—or space—for words for a very long time.

Happy is the bride the sun shines on…

But it wasn't sunny, Addie thought in satisfaction as she gazed out her bedroom window down to the beach below. The sea was covered in morning mist.

It was a far, far different wedding than the last one she'd tried.

They'd decided on a morning wedding because that's when Sophie and their newest addition to their family, Giles William, were at their most social.

They were being social now. Sophie was Noah's decreed 'best man'. She was dressed in so many pink flounces they almost enveloped her. She'd been practising for days, twirling and twirling, loving the way her dress flared when she spun, giggling at the sight of her pink self in the long mirror. It had been hard keeping it fresh but from today she could wear it whenever she wanted.

From today...

It really wasn't from today, Addie thought dreamily as Heidi fussed over her frock.

Addie was wearing a gorgeous, sapphire and white dress, fifties style with a rainbow-coloured shawl. Her dress hugged her to the waist, then flared out as Sophie's did, so they could twirl together. Still breast feeding, her bust was two sizes larger than the last time she'd tried on a wedding dress.

She was a different woman from last time she'd worn a wedding dress.

She was totally, gloriously happy.

For, marriage or not, she and Noah were now permanent in every sense of the word. Currawong seemed to be their for ever home. They were still living in the doctors' house but a beautiful new home was being built up on the headland. They had friends. They had jobs they loved.

They had each other.

Noah…

He was waiting now, dressed in a charcoal suit, standing on the sand with his hand tucked into Sophie's. Sophie…a gloriously contented little girl, her dad's friend.

Her dad? That was now definite. The adoption papers had come through three days after Giles was born. Giles, who was currently being held by Morvena. Morvena was standing with Daisy by her side. Waiting.

It seemed the whole town was waiting.

The promise was for heat later, but right now the sun was struggling to filter golden light through the haze hanging over the ocean. The sea itself was calm and still. Tiny waves washed in and out at the water's edge. Sandpipers scuttled along the shore, feeding at low tide, seemingly oblivious to the chairs, the ribbons, the flower-strewn makeshift altar and the myriad people waiting to see Noah and Addie married.

Any minute now…

She looked at her reflection one last time and her reflection smiled back at her. This was no bride turned out to be someone she wasn't. This was Addie. Mother of Sophie and Giles and a dog called Daisy. This was Addie, obstetrician to Currawong Bay.

This was Addie, beloved of Noah.

She turned from her reflection and Heidi smiled. 'Ready?'

'Ready,' Addie whispered, and smiled and smiled. And then she left her bedroom, she left the house and she walked the last few steps to the beach.

Where Noah stood waiting. Smiling. Her beautiful Noah.

'Will you take this man…?'

Of course she would. Of course she did.

Rings were exchanged, golden bands set with

tiny slivers of agate. They matched the signet ring on Noah's right hand and the simple stone at Addie's throat, jet-black agate with the purest of white hearts.

They were just…right.

Finally the words were spoken. 'I now declare you man and wife,' and Addie's smile couldn't be contained.

And neither could the sun. It broke through the mist in a glorious shaft of golden light, to shine on bride and groom and all who loved them.

Happy is the bride the sun shines on…

But who needs the sun? Addie thought mistily. *Not when I have Noah and Sophie and Giles and Daisy.*

Not when I have everything I need.

Not when I have love.

* * * * *